THE WHISPERED
WATCHWORD

The Famous JUDY BOLTON *Mystery Stories*

By MARGARET SUTTON

In Order of Publication

A Judy Bolton Mystery

THE WHISPERED WATCHWORD

By

Margaret Sutton

Amereon House

To the Reader

It is our pleasure to keep available uncommon titles and
to this end, at the time of publication, we have used the
best available sources. To aid catalogers and collectors,
this title is printed in an edition limited to 80 copies. It
has been manufactured in the United States to American
Library Association standards on permanent, durable,
acid-free paper.　　　　　　　　——— Enjoy!

To order, contact
Amereon House,
the publishing division of
Amereon Ltd.
Post Office Box 1200
Mattituck, New York 11952-9500

To
YOUNG AMERICANS
everywhere
especially those who visit
our nation's Capital
this book
is lovingly dedicated

"Don't open that door!" a voice barked

Contents

x   Contents

CHAPTER I

Through the Passageway

THE Beetle, with Judy and Peter in the front seat and Blackberry, their cat, curled lazily next to the back window, sped toward Washington.

"We're nearly there. Oh, look!" cried Judy as a tall shaft loomed in the distance. "Isn't that the Washington Monument? Why are we stopping, Peter? We aren't going to stay here, are we?"

"I hope we are." Peter had stopped in front of a large motel on the outskirts of the Capital. He glanced apprehensively at Blackberry. Then he grinned—that impish, little-boy grin that Judy loved. "I don't know where else they'd let us stay with Blackberry along as a passenger. Very few hotels allow guests to keep dogs,

1

and I don't know of any other place where a cat would be welcome. This motel won't be bad once we're settled," he added as they got out of the car. "Most of the rooms face an inside court with grass and trees and flower beds. It even has a swimming pool. Shall we go in?"

"In the pool?" asked Judy, laughing. "I would like to go for a dip before it gets dark. We can see the sights this evening. You've been here before, but I—"

"I know, Angel," Peter interrupted gently. "I'm sorry our other trip had to be postponed, but that's the way it is. Uncle Sam's orders come first."

"That's the way it should be," agreed Judy. "I'll understand your work better after I've toured FBI headquarters, but I think I'd like to see the Capitol Building first."

"Then you shall," Peter said, pushing open the front door of the motel.

Inside, the lobby looked bright and cheerful. To Judy, used as she was to country living, the furnishings appeared almost too modern. The chairs, the lamps— everything had a streamlined look. The color scheme was red, white, and blue and there were golden eagles peering down from the walls almost as if they were watching her.

"Those eagles—" she began.

"Don't you like them?" Peter asked. "Patriotic, you know. The good old American eagle."

"Do eagles stand for patriotism?"

Peter considered Judy's question for a moment before he answered. They were waiting at the desk for the clerk to finish registering an impatient young man who had come in just ahead of them. He glanced at Judy as she said the word *eagles* and then looked away. Somehow, Judy didn't like that suspicious glance.

"I want one of your best outside suites. You know, three or four connecting rooms," he said to the clerk in a low voice.

"Your wife has already reserved a room for you."

"No. No." Now the young man seemed extremely nervous. "The rooms aren't for us. I was asked to reserve them. I'll pay for them in advance." He withdrew a large bill from his pocket and placed it on the counter. "May I have the keys now?" he asked. "The people will be along later. They're here for a business conference. You understand?"

"Yes, of course." The clerk mentioned the numbers of the rooms and indicated an open book on the counter. "If you sign for them it will be all right."

The young man signed his name, took the keys, and departed hurriedly. Judy saw him flash a smile to the girl at the switchboard just before he went out through a rear door. Beyond, in an enclosed area, she could see trees, benches, and a swimming pool complete with diving board and a wading pool for little children. It was crowded now. Perhaps later, after they had unpacked their things, she and Peter could go for a swim. Peter signed the register, *Mr. and Mrs. Peter Dobbs, Roulsville, Pennsylvania,* and, to Judy's surprise, asked for an outside suite, mentioning the number.

"But Peter, what about Blackberry?" she protested. "I thought we'd take a room where we could just open the door the way we do at home and let him out into the garden. Those rooms on the court—"

"We may move into one of them tomorrow. We're all set for tonight," Peter broke in with a look she knew from past experience. It meant that he would explain later. She said, "About the eagles? You were telling me—"

"I believe they stand for courage. They came down to us from the Greeks and Romans, possibly from the ancient Egyptians." Peter's fund of information always amazed Judy. "A great many countries use them on their coins and on their national emblems," he continued. "There's the black eagle of Germany and the two-headed Russian eagle. Mexico has an eagle on its coat of arms. There's a picture of it in the dictionary at home."

"Do you mean that eagle with a snake in its beak?" Judy asked with a shudder.

"That's the one. The snake is symbolic of the evil that must be crushed out of any government. I like our American eagle better," declared Peter. "He carries a banner with *E Pluribus Unum* printed on it."

" 'Out of many, one,' " Judy said thoughtfully. "I like it better, too. There are a lot of problems to be brought up in Congress this summer, aren't there? I'd like to sit in on some of the sessions."

"I can arrange that," Peter said. "Senator Hockett may make some recommendation on federal control of underworld rackets," he continued. "Crime is big business in this country. You might call it the snake our eagle has to kill. The senator's committee is investigating a secret organization—"

"That sounds interesting!" Judy interrupted with a little squeal of excitement. "I love secrets."

"You don't love this kind," Peter told her gravely.

Blackberry was still sleeping next to the rear window when they returned to the car. Peter drove it around to a parking place just outside the room they had taken.

"Convenient, isn't it?" he commented. "You could make a quick getaway from here."

"Who wants to make a quick getaway?" she asked. "An inside room would be quieter, and there would be a place for Blackberry to roam. He's apt to get run over if we let him out here."

"You're right about that," Peter agreed, looking at the double row of parked cars before the long motel buildings. "But there must be a passageway—"

"There is," Judy said. "See, there's a porter wheeling

a hand truck through it now. It must lead to those inside rooms and the swimming pool."

"More likely it leads to the laundry. That's soiled linen in the truck," observed Peter.

"Oh, I hope not." Judy loved long passageways. She felt sure this one must lead somewhere exciting, and started off with Blackberry in her arms.

There were noises in the passageway that frightened Blackberry. A sound, as of something heavy being lowered, increased, then stopped. Thump! Quiet and then another thump.

"Giants walking!" thought Judy with a shiver.

Looking back, she could see the reassuring line of cars parked outside the motel. The Beetle was squeezed in between a car from Illinois and another one from Ohio. Peter was out there checking off license numbers when Judy glanced back at him.

Ahead, the passageway took a turn past a machine that delivered ice cubes. Beyond, just as Judy had hoped, was the enclosed garden with the pool in the center. Finding a secluded spot, she deposited Blackberry in a bed of geraniums and looked around.

The motel spread over an entire city block. Each room had its own private entrance. The upper rooms opened out on a balcony that ran the length of the long buildings to the right and left of the enclosed garden.

"An inside room would have been nice," Judy thought.

In front of her, as she faced the main building, was an open terrace which proved to be an extension of the motel dining room. The young man she had observed when they registered was sitting alone at an outdoor table covered with a gay plaid tablecloth. Judy noticed the expression on his face was far from gay. Presently he was joined by a husky young man with blond hair, and the two of them left through the passageway Judy had taken.

She picked up Blackberry and was about to follow them when suddenly the cat objected. He leaped from her arms and dashed across the walk that led to the swimming pool, nearly tripping one of the bathers. The girl skidded to a stop, and a woman, evidently her mother, called sharply, "Watch yourself, Rosita! Who would let a cat in here? Today you are unlucky. Today I must watch."

"That's foolish, Mamma. I don't see why you have to watch me all the time. I never have any fun. Just because a black cat ran across my path—"

"Foolish, is it?" interrupted her mother. "Your papa is foolish. He will not pay. I warn you, Rosita. They will try, maybe, to push you from a window. Maybe a car is coming. I tell you, they will make it look just like an accident!"

Judy listened, horrified. She had Blackberry now. She wouldn't let him go again, not when that woman was around. Young people were leaving the swimming pool by twos and threes, disappearing through the different doors. They were not paying any attention to the frightened girl and her mother. Judy smiled sympathetically at Rosita just before her mother hurried her through another door.

Over each door was a number and a golden eagle. A corresponding number was on the tag attached to each door key. The number on Judy's key was easy to remember. What she didn't remember was the direction she took at the turn there by the ice dispenser. Was it right or left? Uncertain, she stood holding Blackberry and listening.

"What *is* that noise?" she wondered as the thumping came again, more distinctly.

The air in the passageway was misty. That gave her a clue. She had just about decided what the noise was when she heard a voice say: "It must look like an accident. *You* will see to that. If you want to live—"

That was all Judy wanted to hear. Panic seized her. Running the length of the passageway, she found a door at the end. Impulsively, she opened it and then stood frozen as a ghostly object loomed up in front of her.

CHAPTER II

An Unusual Ghost

"WHAT do you want?" a voice asked out of the mist.

"Excuse me. I—I'm sorry," gasped Judy, still staring at the moving white object. She could see what it was now. Obviously, she had opened the door to the laundry room. The woman operating a shirt-pressing machine stopped long enough to exclaim, "Glory be! We don't wash cats here, miss. You must have taken a wrong turn."

"Yes, I—I guess I did."

Still Judy stared at the machine. The shirt, looming up like a ghost, was practically ironing itself. The sleeves were stretched out mechanically, then pressed with a thumping sound as the huge ironing machine

9

came down on them. That was the little thump Judy had heard when she was standing in the passageway. The giant thump was when the back of the shirt was pressed. The whole operation took no more than a minute.

"Wonderful, isn't it?" the operator asked, her eyes twinkling with amusement.

"Terrifying is the word for it," replied Judy, "especially if you come upon it unexpectedly. It sounds like giants walking from out there in the passageway, and it looks—"

"I know. Like a headless ghost."

"Exactly," agreed Judy. "I heard voices, too. Did you hear anyone saying anything about an accident?"

"You can't hear much when the pressers are going. Besides, we don't have accidents here," the woman replied. "Mr. Rocklin, the motel manager, sees to that. Maybe you heard him talking with someone in the office."

"Is the office next to the laundry?"

"What's that?" The pressing machine had come down with a thump. The operator had not heard Judy's question.

"The office," she shouted, her voice sounding too loud in the silence that followed the thump.

"Over there!" A hand holding another shirt indicated the direction. "Entrance is from the lobby."

Judy murmured, "Thank you," as she turned to go,

but felt sure it went unheard. The pressing machine was making another ghost out of the shirt in the operator's hand. Blackberry's tail bristled as Judy hurried away with him.

Peter found her experience in the laundry very amusing when she told him about it. She was laughing now. It made her forget how frightened she had been.

"I might have known you were off chasing ghosts," he said with a chuckle. "Blackberry's tail is still twice its natural size. Put him down and take a look at our living quarters complete with red, white, and blue draw drapes and an air conditioner under the window. It has all the comforts of home and a few extras. It's patriotic, too. There are eagles everywhere, even in the wall paper."

"I could do without the eagles, but I do like the room," Judy admitted, trying one of the blue chairs. Peter sat down on a red one.

"Comfortable," he said. "Nice for watching television in the evening if we have nothing else to do. All the rooms are equipped with television sets. Try it and see if the picture's clear."

The picture was clear. So was the sound. A voice boomed out at Judy. "This is your last chance. Accidents happen . . ."

"A gangster picture," she remarked, turning off the set. "I'm not in the mood to watch it."

"Not scared, I hope?"

"Not when I know it's television," Judy replied. "But something I overheard just before I stumbled into the laundry scared me. Maybe part of it was a television program," Judy added dubiously, "but somehow I didn't think so. Maybe this woman I met had been frightened by some program. I don't know. I only know she was frightened, and so was her daughter. They seemed to be expecting some sort of an accident to happen. The girl looked about twelve years old, and yet the mother watched her like a baby. She was upset because Blackberry crossed her daughter's path. I'm afraid he isn't going to be very popular with the guests, Peter. I almost wish we'd left him with the people who rented our house in Dry Brook Hollow."

"If you want to leave him somewhere, I know of a better place." Peter laughed and spread a copy of the *Washington Daily News* before Judy's astonished eyes. He pointed out a statement made by Senator Hockett. The senator's secret investigation of underworld crime, the news item said, had uncovered the fact that mice were overrunning the basement of the Old Senate Office Building.

"Since the beauty parlor for the lady staff members of the Senate is in the basement," the news item continued, "there has been widespread feminine distress. Senator Hockett reports that the situation is intolerable. These bold, brazen underworld characters are turning hair-dos into scare-dos."

"Oh, that's funny!" Judy exclaimed. "Or is it? Horace writes this way when he wants to hold some public figure up to ridicule. You know. Like Kay Vincent's father when he was running for mayor of Farringdon. That brother of mine really showed him up. But why would anyone want to make fun of Senator Hockett?"

"He has his enemies," Peter said reflectively. "A great many people are afraid the states will lose some of their rights if the federal government has any more power. And yet crime must be controlled. It's too easy, the way the law is now, for a criminal syndicate to extend its operations over a number of states without breaking any federal law. Senator Hockett wants the facts. Then he will make some recommendation to Congress."

"I would like to be there when he makes it," declared Judy. "I've seen his picture in the paper. Big glasses. Big smile. He looks like a man who likes cats. Peter, do you really think he'd want to keep Blackberry? I mean just until the mice are eliminated?"

"Blackberry is the one to eliminate them. He did a pretty good job of eliminating the mice in our barn at home," declared Peter. "You might offer his services to the senator."

"Me?" Judy questioned. "Are you suggesting that I go up to Senator Hockett's office with a cat in my arms? Wouldn't he laugh?"

"Probably. They do call him the smiling senator.

You'll have to get a pass at his office anyway if you want a seat in the senate gallery," Peter reminded her. "Just tell him you're one of his constituents. You will be voting one of these days . . ."

"That's right. I will." Judy was suddenly lost in thought, not hearing the rest of what Peter was saying. Voting for the first time was an important step. She wanted to know enough about politics to vote intelligently. Meeting the senator would help. As for offering Blackberry, she didn't know. "Let me think about it a little longer," she said. "I can't do it until tomorrow, anyway. By then I'll be able to decide."

"You might write a letter for Blackberry," Peter suggested, walking over to a built-in desk and beginning to write on a piece of motel stationery. "You might say that, as a public-spirited *catstituent*, he offers himself—"

"No, his services," Judy objected, laughing at the new word Peter had invented. "You said yourself that it's only his services as a mouse-catcher that he will be offering. If you're writing a letter for him you ought to tell the senator that Blackberry guarantees to make the beauty parlor *purrfectly* safe for lady staff members. It's funny, but I never thought of a beauty parlor in the basement of the Capitol. I wonder what else is there."

"Wonder girl," Peter teased her. "You'll soon find out. I know there's a subway there. The senators ride their own private subway to the office building across Constitution Avenue."

"Will I ride the subway, too? I suppose it goes through a long, underground passageway. I hope it won't be as spooky as the passageway through this building," Judy said with a shiver. "I can still hear that evil voice saying something must look like an accident. Maybe it was somebody's television, but it didn't sound like it. Peter, I mean it. It sounded like the real thing."

"Exactly where were you standing when you heard it?" Peter questioned.

"I'll show you on our way to the swimming pool. You are going in for a dip before dinner, aren't you?" Judy asked.

Peter seemed more interested in the passageway than in the pool. "You might mention what you heard to Senator Hockett when you offer Blackberry's services," he suggested. "I have a few telephone calls to make after we've had our swim, and then we'll be free to go exploring. How would you like to tour the Capitol grounds tonight?"

"I'd love it," agreed Judy, her worries about the voices in the passageway momentarily forgotten.

CHAPTER III

A Missing "Catstituent"

AN HOUR later, refreshed after a dip in the pool and a quick snack in the motel restaurant, Judy and Peter were ready to leave. Blackberry looked so comfortable on top of the desk in their room that they decided to let him stay there.

"He will be all right. After all," Peter said with a laugh, "he does have his letter to write. We'll drive downtown and park the car and walk around. You'd like that, wouldn't you, Angel?"

"Oh, yes," replied Judy. "I'd love it. 'Bye, Blackberry," she said airily as they went out. "His turn to see the Capitol will come tomorrow, won't it, Peter? I think he's going to like that basement full of mice."

"I see you've decided to offer his services to the senator. Will you tell him what a famous cat he is?" asked Peter as he led the way past the other parked cars to where he had left the Beetle.

"I may." Judy settled herself in the seat beside him. She was thinking of Blackberry's fame and wondering, as she often did, how much of it was due to the cat's superior intelligence and how much to chance. A life-saving medal decorated the collar he wore. That might make an impression on Senator Hockett. Or wasn't he the sort of man to be impressed by medals? Judy was eager to meet him. She wasn't sure just yet how much she would tell him.

"I hope Blackberry will be all right alone in our room," Peter said suddenly, speaking Judy's own thoughts as if he had read them. She had tried not to show her uneasiness, but it was no use.

"We won't be gone long," she said reassuringly. "That folder they gave us when we registered says it only takes five minutes to drive to the Capitol."

"I doubt if we'll get there that fast," Peter replied. He was driving down New York Avenue, a busy street twinkling with neon signs. Judy would have the car to herself the following day, and he wanted her to be sure of the direction. "You may find Washington a little confusing," he told her. "There are so many little parks and monuments with streets branching out from them like the spokes of so many wheels. The numbered streets run north and south. The lettered streets run east and west. It's these streets named after states that are apt to confuse you. Take New York Avenue, for instance. It crosses Pennsylvania at the White House. If we turn on New Jersey we'll be on our way to the Capitol."

"Let's turn then," Judy suggested.

Peter made a left turn. He pointed out the government printing office and a few other buildings as they passed them, but Judy's eyes were on the dome of the Capitol, shining white under the floodlights. A single light gleamed from the lantern above. Peter said that indicated that Congress was in session. It could be a meeting of one or both houses.

"That statue at the very top represents Freedom," he continued when he had parked the car on a tree-lined street just north of the Capitol. "Shall we walk over and pay her a visit?"

Most of the statues they had seen so far were of men. There were big statues and little statues hidden in the shrubbery. They came upon a huge statue unexpectedly, and Judy let out a little shriek of excitement.

"Who is it?" she gasped, clutching Peter's arm.

A towering shaft not far from where they had parked the car housed the bigger-than-life statue at its base. It must be a statue of Washington or some other great President. Judy was surprised when Peter told her it was a statue of the late Senator Taft.

"It is? I didn't think senators were that important," Judy murmured.

"It depends on the senator. Anyway," Peter added, "you can't tell the importance of a man by the size of his monument. Shall we do some more exploring?"

"Yes, let's." This was what Judy had been waiting for. The light in the dome of the Capitol went out. She and Peter watched a few of the senators and congressmen leave. There were only a few.

"Most of them leave from the other entrance," Peter explained.

"I don't see why. This entrance is so beautiful."

Everything about the Capitol Building thrilled Judy. It was partly hidden by the magnificent trees that dotted the spacious grounds. The Washington Elm, more than a hundred feet high, and other trees nearly as old, were marked with small metal plaques which Judy had difficulty reading in the dark.

Other couples strolled past them. Judy paid little attention to them. She had so many questions to ask Peter as they walked. He pointed out the north, or Senate, extension of the Capitol Building and the south extension that housed the Hall of Representatives.

"You'll see the old hall when you take the tour tomorrow," he added.

"Will I have to tour the inside of the Capitol Building all by myself?" asked Judy.

"I can't be there tomorrow, Angel," Peter said regretfully. "I'll be busy at the Bureau. But take the guided tour, and you won't feel lonely. And I'll meet you for lunch."

Judy said she would. She was eager to explore everything. Tonight, with Peter, was her best night. No tour with strangers could be as thrilling as this.

"It must be late," Peter said finally. "Shall we go home and come back tomorrow?"

"Home?" Judy laughed at the term. "Do you call

that motel room home? I almost dread going back. If it wasn't for Blackberry there alone . . ."

Her voice trailed off. They were back at the Capitol steps. Long steps always tempted her.

"Peter," she announced suddenly, "I want to walk up the Capitol steps and down again. Do you mind?"

Peter didn't mind at all. They counted the steps, like children, and found that there were just one hundred of them. From the top they had a magnificent view of the Washington Monument to the west where a green mall dotted with shrubbery extended all the way to the

Lincoln Memorial on the banks of the Potomac. Water glistened from an oblong pool, reflecting lights and shadows. It was all so quiet and beautiful. They descended slowly. Judy was still reluctant to leave.

"I know it's late, but I want to do some more exploring. Those buildings way over there look like castles. What are they?" she asked wonderingly.

"Museums and art galleries," replied Peter. "You'll see them all tomorrow after we've had lunch. There's a fountain inside the Department of Justice Building. I'll meet you there at twelve-thirty."

"I'll be there," Judy promised. "I can hardly wait. Look, Peter!" she exclaimed as they continued their walk. "Are those statues or little stone houses there in the shrubbery?"

"They're grottos," Peter said, following her glance.

"What's in them?"

"Fountains, I think. Let's have a look."

Both grottos were closed. Peter pushed against what looked as if it might be the door to the one on the right. It didn't give an inch. And yet, as they turned away, Judy had the strangest feeling that something alive was moving around behind it.

"I'm sure I heard something," she insisted.

"A squirrel, probably," Peter reassured her. "There are bound to be squirrels around with so many trees."

"It didn't sound like a squirrel. I suppose a catbird could be calling from one of those bushes. Do they call at night, or am I just nervous thinking of Blackberry there in the room alone?"

"You are nervous."

Judy was shivering although the night was warm. Peter was walking on her left. Did his footsteps echo on the walk behind him? A tall statue stood in the little circular garden at Judy's right. She glanced at it, and Peter began to laugh. He had heard footsteps, too. He pointed out a man in uniform patrolling the Capitol grounds.

"Secret Service?" Judy questioned.

Peter nodded. "You didn't think that statue over there decided it needed a little exercise, did you?"

"How did you guess? Oh, Peter!" Judy moved closer to him. "There are so many statues. It makes me feel that more of our great men are dead than living. What's that statue up ahead?"

"It's Peace. Symbolic, you know. Men are still working for Peace and Freedom. All these statues are symbolic of the values these men cherished. Think of them that way and they won't scare you," Peter advised. "Now shall we go?"

This time Judy was willing. They took the shortest route back to the motel and arrived there just as a clock in the distance was striking twelve.

"Midnight!" Judy said with a shiver. "I'm glad we left when we did. I'm sure those statues walk at midnight."

"Something does!" Peter's voice was grim. "I'm afraid it walked right into our apartment."

"Oh, Peter!" Judy cried in distress as they entered. "We left Blackberry inside, and now he's out. Who do you suppose opened the door?"

"Someone with a key. We locked the door when we left." Peter looked about the large room hopefully while Judy investigated the smaller dressing room and the adjoining bath.

"He isn't here!" they both exclaimed in the same breath. And then, because Blackberry's disappearance seemed so final, they stood as still as statues themselves gazing at the empty desk top where they had left him.

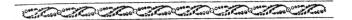

CHAPTER IV

A Strange Message

PETER was the first to notice a difference in the appearance of the room. The golden eagle on the wall was crooked, and the desk was clear. It had been strewn with papers when Judy and Peter left for their tour of the Capitol grounds. Now it was clear of everything except the motel stationery and a glass paperweight placed squarely on top of the blank sheets of paper.

"They're all blank. That's strange," Judy observed. "Where's that letter you were writing for Blackberry? You know, all that nonsense about him being a catstituent. Why would anybody take that?"

"It didn't blow away," declared Peter. "I left this glass paperweight on top of it."

The paperweight was one that had been on the desk when they arrived. It was a plain rectangle with a picture of the Capitol pasted on the bottom so that it showed through the glass. Fingerprints on the paperweight could be detected in the FBI laboratory. They might be a clue to Blackberry's disappearance, but Judy doubted it.

"There could be dozens of fingerprints. People are in and out of a motel room like this almost every night. The maids must lift the paperweight when they dust the desk. They take care of the rooms. Wait!" Judy stopped herself. "There's an idea. The maids have keys, don't they? Maybe they heard Blackberry yowling in here. He does yowl sometimes when he feels trapped, and I'm sure he would feel trapped in a little room like this when he's used to so much space. They could have let him out. Maybe if I call—"

"Try it," Peter suggested.

Opening the door which they had closed so carefully behind them, Judy took a deep breath. A cat could hide under one of the many cars now crowded in the parking space between the long buildings. Blackberry always came the minute he heard Judy's voice.

"Kitty! Kitty! Nice kitty!" she began calling.

"Here, Blackberry!" Peter joined in, calling the cat as if he were a dog.

They called and called. Blackberry always came to either call when he was within hearing distance.

"He could be trapped somewhere," Peter suggested. He glanced upward. Hopefully, Judy followed his glance. A railed balcony ran the full length of the long building. It reminded her of the porch across the front of their home in Dry Brook Hollow. Maybe it had seemed familiar to Blackberry, too.

"I'm going up there and call," Judy announced suddenly.

Peter started to protest that people might be sleeping, but Judy's persistent "Kitty! Kitty!" interrupted him.

Presently one of the upper doors opened.

"Can't you be quiet out there?" someone called. Judy didn't see who it was. She didn't know any of the people in the motel, anyway. It was a man's voice. He sounded angry. A woman's head popped out of another door.

"We could all use a little quiet around here," she complained. "First it was the cat, and now you—"

"The cat?" Judy interrupted. "Did you hear it?"

"I sure did," she replied, "and so did the manager's wife. Her cousin let it out."

"How long ago was that?" asked Peter. He had vaulted up the steps as soon as he heard the voices.

"Couple of hours. Maybe longer. That Mrs. Rocklin's a character," the woman volunteered. She seemed to have forgotten that it was after midnight, and went on about Mrs. Rocklin until, quite suddenly, it dawned on Judy that Mrs. Rocklin must be the mother of the little girl by the swimming pool.

"Does she have a daughter?" Judy interrupted to ask.

"Sure. Nice kid, too. I think they call her Rosalie or something like that. She was crying and telling her cousin he shouldn't have let the cat out. I'm telling you, for a motel that's supposed to be so quiet and peaceful—"

"It will be quiet and peaceful again," Peter broke in, "if you will just tell us where we can find the cat."

"The girl had it in her arms the last I saw of it. She was running as fast as she could run. Her mother and the cousin went after her, and then things quieted down for a spell. I heard Rosie calling, 'Papa!' and after that we had a little peace."

"Her father is the motel manager, Peter. Maybe we can find out more at the desk," Judy suggested.

She was eager to get away from the angry man and the talkative woman, but Peter had a few more questions to ask. He was curious about Mrs. Rocklin's cousin. If he opened the door simply to let the cat out, why would he disturb any of the papers on the desk?

"That puzzles me, too," Judy admitted. "Let's ask the manager himself."

Although it was after midnight, the desk clerk was busy when Judy and Peter walked into the lobby. More tourists had arrived. They were just signing the register when Peter stepped up to ask for the manager.

"His office is over there," he was told. The clerk indicated a door across the lobby. Judy and Peter walked over to it and rapped. Receiving no answer, they tried the door and found it locked.

"Naturally he isn't in at this hour. We'll have to come back in the morning," Peter said.

Morning seemed a long time to wait for news of Blackberry. Judy glanced at the clerk. Maybe he would know something. He was at the switchboard now, replacing the girl who had been there in the daytime. Judy had never thought about it before, but suddenly it occurred to her that operating a hotel switchboard might be an interesting job. A switchboard operator would know all about what went on in a motel. She told Peter her idea, and he said it would do no harm to ask.

"We had a cat with us," he began, walking over to the switchboard.

"A big black one?" the clerk asked.

"Yes, that's the one. Did you see him?" Judy questioned eagerly.

"*Hear* him is more like it. The switchboard was buzzing with complaints. I thought you'd ask about him. There's a note in your box . . ."

"Let's have it, please."

Peter read the message and handed it to Judy. It said:
DOGS, CATS, AND OTHER PETS ARE NOT ALLOWED IN THE
ROOMS. IF THEY SENT YOU TO FRIGHTEN US WITH YOUR

CAT IT WILL NOT WORK. THE CAT WAS RETURNED AND YOUR MAN WAS PAID FOR THE LAST TIME. IF THIS IS A FREE COUNTRY IT MUST BE FREE FOR HONEST PEOPLE TO MAKE A LIVING. THREATS TO SENATOR HOCKETT WILL NOT HELP. HE IS DETERMINED TO STOP YOU. I AM DETERMINED ALSO.

The message was signed *Anthony Rocklin.*

Judy read it for a second time, puzzling over it. Finally she said in bewilderment, "Peter, he thinks we were sent here on purpose to frighten him. Who does he think sent us?"

"When we find out," Peter replied grimly, "we will know where Blackberry is. Probably he's safe. They're not after cats. They're after people."

Judy was shocked into silence for a moment. Then she said, "I suppose I should be grateful. Blackberry may help us solve this mystery the way he's helped us so many times before. I was afraid they had let him out into all that traffic on New York Avenue. Now it's Rosita's safety that worries me. I'm beginning to see why her mother watches her every minute. But if Mr. Rocklin paid, the way the note said, she's no longer in danger, is she?"

"I'm afraid it isn't that simple."

"No?" Judy had been sure it wouldn't be. Rosita must still be watched. Freedom must still be denied her, although she had enjoyed a few minutes of it running with the cat. Judy could just imagine Mrs. Rocklin

The eagle was hinged like a locket

screaming at her. Now she could understand the mother's fear. Mr. Rocklin's note had explained much. What was it he had said about freedom?

IF THIS IS A FREE COUNTRY IT MUST BE FREE FOR HONEST PEOPLE TO MAKE A LIVING. That was true. But there was something else in the message that puzzled Judy.

"What do you think Mr. Rocklin meant by threats to Senator Hockett?" she asked. "Did he think that ridiculous letter you started to write was meant as a threat?"

"Perhaps." Peter's answer was brief. He seemed preoccupied with his own thoughts as they walked back to their room.

"Our neighbors are still up," observed Judy, noticing a light in the room next to theirs. "I hope they don't talk all night and keep us awake. It's bad enough to have those eagles—"

"To tell you the truth, I'm a little suspicious of them myself," Peter admitted. "I reached up to straighten that one on the wall, and it came apart in my hand."

"How could it come apart?"

"Like this!" Peter demonstrated. The eagle was not solid. It was hinged, like a locket, and the inside would have made an excellent hiding place. It was empty, of course. The whole room seemed empty and desolate without Blackberry.

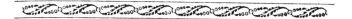

CHAPTER V

On the Stairway

"PETER, it's nearly eight o'clock!" Judy exclaimed. She was up ahead of Peter, suddenly aware that they had both overslept. "Aren't you supposed to be at the Department of Justice Building at nine? Wake up, sleepyhead! We forgot to set the alarm."

Blackberry was usually their alarm. At home Judy always put him out. Then he would yowl to come in at the crack of dawn. But this morning, where was he? What kind of a night had he spent?

"I suppose some criminals are kind to animals," Judy said thoughtfully as she brushed her hair. "Peter," she called in to the bathroom where he was shaving, "isn't there time to put an ad in the paper for Blackberry before we leave?"

"I'll take care of that. Don't worry about it," advised Peter. "I want you to enjoy your tour of the Capital. If you do meet Senator Hockett, you might tell him what we planned."

"What's the use?" sighed Judy. "We can't lend Blackberry to him now."

"No, but it's just possible he knows who's behind this protection racket," Peter said. "That's what I meant when I said crime is big business. A hotel owner like Mr. Rocklin needs all kinds of services and supplies. If a crime syndicate has moved in on him, he may be forced to pay what the gangsters call protection."

"And if he doesn't pay—"

"Then there's trouble. The mob may try to frighten him. A cat yowling in one of the rooms might drive away a few guests and serve as a warning. That's why Blackberry was given to the mobsters. Mr. Rocklin apparently thought they had planted him."

"But *they* knew they didn't, Peter."

"Yes, but we may have given them an idea, though. They may plant Blackberry again as a second warning. Or the mob may use violence. Most of the people who are terrorized in this way are afraid to report any threats to the authorities because of reprisals. They remember a Chicago restaurant owner who cooperated with a Senate committee investigating crime and paid for it dearly. Armed thugs entered his place, poured gasoline on the floor and burned down the restaurant."

"That sounds like some of the stories Mrs. Rocklin was telling Rosita. Weren't they caught?" asked Judy.

Peter shook his head. "They seldom are. Fear moves in along with the mob. Nobody will talk. I know exactly what would happen if I identified myself as a government agent and questioned Mr. Rocklin. He would say nothing."

"But the message?"

"He thought we were working for the syndicate. I'm convinced that's why he left it. That note says more than you know."

"It doesn't say where Blackberry is."

"No," Peter replied cheerfully, "but it gives us a clue. I'm convinced he's safe. His collar will prove he's no ordinary cat. The mobster may return him to collect a reward."

"But our home address is on his collar," Judy objected.

"All the better," Peter said. "They will realize the cat belongs to a tourist staying at Mr. Rocklin's motel. I'll put a notice in the Washington papers offering a big reward and then see what happens. We've set traps before. With Uncle Sam's help, I'm sure Blackberry will be catching mice in the basement of the Capitol before the week is over."

"I hope so." Judy sighed deeply. It was only partly a sigh of relief. She was thinking of the problems of the Rocklin family and trying to see what had happened as they would see it. Family problems were her department, Peter said. He'd take care of the note.

"Question Rosita, if you have the chance, and report back to me," he advised Judy. "There's something strange going on in this motel. It isn't anything we can handle all by ourselves, either. We're going to need plenty of help."

Judy knew what he meant. She glanced uneasily at the expensive cars in the parking lot. Motor courts like this were usually less crowded in the daytime.

The cars were the same ones Judy had seen Peter checking the night before. Laundry carts piled with fresh linen were being wheeled from the laundry room. Judy thought of the voice she had heard in the passageway and shivered. It frightened her all the more because she had heard voices talking all night in the room next to theirs, and one had sounded so much like the voice in the passageway. She mentioned this to Peter, and he answered as if he already knew.

"That room backs up against the passageway to the laundry. So does this one," he added.

"Did you figure that out last night? Did you stay awake and listen to what was said?" Judy asked in amazement.

"I didn't stay awake." Again his answer was brief. It silenced Judy. Peter knew something he wasn't free to tell her, but she didn't care. She had learned not to pry. The answers would come in time. In the meantime she would try to enjoy her tour of the Capitol just as if nothing had happened.

"The guide will show you all through the building for a quarter and still leave you time for a little exploring by yourself," Peter was saying when they were on their way.

"I wish you could be my guide," Judy replied wistfully. "I still don't like the thought of doing all my sightseeing alone."

"That's just it," Peter told her. "You won't be alone. Everybody else will be sightseeing, too. This is the time of year that graduating classes from all over the country plan their trips to Washington. You may even meet someone from Farringdon or Roulsville."

Judy doubted it. Her class didn't take the usual Washington trip, she remembered. All the money they raised went toward furnishings for the new school after the old one burned. Just thinking of that dear old school being licked by flames made Judy shudder. It had been like losing a friend. And yet she remembered a time when it had seemed as strange to her as the buildings in Washington did now. Statues and monuments were everywhere. Judy had seen some of them in pictures. A queer feeling took hold of her as if the picture postcards Peter used to send her when he was studying to become a G-man had suddenly come to life.

"I've seen that monument on a postcard," Judy remarked as Peter drove past Mount Vernon Square, taking a different route to show her the sights. She found it a little confusing. This time he turned on Massachusetts Avenue. After a hurried breakfast along the way, he drove on to the Capitol where he parked the car in a space that Judy later noticed was marked RESERVED FOR SENATORS ONLY.

"Remember, twelve-thirty by the fountain," he said as they parted. "You won't mind taking the tour by yourself, will you?"

Judy assured him that she wouldn't. Just the same, when Peter was gone, she found she did mind being alone among strangers. Other tourists seemed to be entering the Capitol in groups. Several students were gazing up at the dome while their teacher pointed out the thirty-six columns supporting it and went on to explain that there were only thirty-six states in the union when the dome of the Capitol was built.

"Inside," she continued, "you will see only sixteen columns supporting the original rotunda in the oldest part of the building when there were sixteen states in the union."

Judy stood listening for a moment, half wishing she could be one of the students. She didn't mind being alone at home, but here with so many people she felt utterly lost. The Capitol looked very different in the daytime. Where were those mysterious grottos and all the shade trees? Then she realized.

"Of course," she reminded herself. "That was the west front of the Capitol. This is the east entrance. No wonder they look different!"

The vast halls of the Capitol Building echoed with footsteps of tourists going back and forth, all so sure of where they were going. Judy didn't know which way to turn. Making inquiry, she found she had just missed the first guided tour.

"There will be another one in ten minutes," she was told.

Instead of paying her quarter and lining up for the next tour, she decided to wander around and really look at things. There was so much to see. Over her head in the great dome was a painting of figures in the clouds. The guide would tell her what they were later. She could see that a great artist must have painted the mural, but it was so high overhead that it hurt her neck to look at it.

On the walls, where they were easier to see, were other murals—the *Landing of the Pilgrims*, *Penn Making a Treaty with the Indians*, and many others. Judy didn't need a guide to tell her they were famous paintings. Once she had overcome that lost feeling, she might be able to step back into history and enjoy them.

The noise of many feet coming down a little stairway attracted her attention. She could hear the guide saying something about this being the stairway the British had used when they set fire to the Capitol in 1814.

That was a bit of history Judy had forgotten. In school she had never found history very interesting. Now she wished she had paid closer attention to her books.

"There was a war in 1812," she remembered. "It must have been during the war that the fire was set."

A crackling noise attracted her attention. For just a moment she imagined herself back in time hearing the crackling of the fire. According to the guide conducting the tour she had just missed, flames had destroyed the interior of both the north and south wings of the original Capitol Building.

"You have just seen Statuary Hall," the guide was saying to a group of school children trooping down the stairs with their harassed teacher. "Back in 1814, when the fire was set, that hall where you saw all the statues was the House of Representatives. A wooden passageway connected it to the Senate wing when the interiors of both buildings were set afire . . ."

"What's that?" exclaimed one of the school children as the crackling noise sounded again.

Judy looked and saw to her amazement that it was Rosita who had spoken. The crackling was nothing but paper being crumpled by one of her classmates, but the fright in Rosita's face was real.

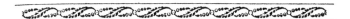

CHAPTER VI

Among the Statues

"Rosita, it's all right," Judy reassured the frightened girl, moving closer to her and standing on a wide stone step where the stairway curved. "That was only one of the children crackling a piece of paper."

"But it sounded like flames crackling, and Mamma said they might set fire—"

"Don't worry about what your mother said," Judy said quietly. "There's no fire."

"I'm glad." Rosita edged over from the narrow end of the step to let the others pass. She huddled against Judy for a moment and then looked up into her face. "They took your cat," she confided. "Papa wouldn't believe me. He said you were one of them."

"Who are they?" asked Judy. "I mean these people who frighten your mother and father. What do they want?"

"Money," the younger girl replied. "Lots of money. They say they'll hurt me if Papa doesn't give it to them. Mamma says he must pay them. She says it's protection —for me. But Papa says it's a free country and he doesn't have to pay protection."

"That's the way it should be."

"But it isn't. They wanted money last night, but my cousin took your cat over there instead. Papa thought it was left in the room on purpose to scare him. They do things like that. That's why Mamma watches me every minute except when I'm in school, and then the teacher watches me. I can't talk any longer because she's watching me now."

"Poor teacher!" Judy sympathized. "She needs eyes in the back of her head."

Rosita laughed. It did Judy's heart good to hear her. But she was soon serious again as she asked, "You do see how it is, don't you?"

"Yes, I see." Judy saw it all too well. Peter had already explained it. Rosita was only confirming what he had told her an hour earlier.

"Papa isn't going to pay them any more," Rosita rushed on, trying to make the most of the little time she had to talk. "He and Mamma were quarreling about it half the night. I'm scared. If he doesn't pay—"

"Who collects this money?" Judy interrupted to ask.

"I don't know his name, but I can find out from Papa. It's a man who owns a restaurant."

"Do you know where this restaurant is?"

"I think I know. I'll find out after school. See you?" Rosita called back as she hurried to join her classmates. The teacher was motioning frantically and saying, "Let's keep together, children."

Feeling like a child herself, Judy continued on up the stone stairway worn by the many feet that had climbed up and down it over the years. She tried to imagine British soldiers creeping stealthily up those same steps to burn the Capitol.

"They could have been my ancestors," she thought, "but then they were the enemy."

It was a comforting thought. Enemies could change into friends. The people of the world could learn to understand each other. Judy had no proof of it, only an abiding faith. It was important to her that the world saw America as a nation with such a faith. Instead of saying, as she had said to Rosita, "That's the way it should be," she wanted to be able to say, "That's the way it is."

In this mood, Judy climbed the worn stairway, passed through the small rotunda with its sixteen columns and entered the former Hall of Representatives, now known as Statuary Hall.

The first tour had been a large one with Rosita's class and perhaps a dozen adults being guided through the Capitol. The second tour had not yet arrived. Judy found the great hall empty except for a few tourists who were wandering around the way she was and the motionless statues that seemed to be gazing down at her from every part of the room.

Some of the statues were in bronze. Some were in marble. Nearly all of them either stood or sat upon tall pedestals with their names and the dates of birth and death engraved upon them. Judy looked around the vast semicircular hall to see if there were any statues of the living. It was an immense room with Corinthian columns of dark Italian marble supporting a domed ceiling. Light came through on the statues in dim, slanting rays.

"It's beautiful," thought Judy, and yet it was a little frightening, too. The marble statues were too white, almost as if the spirits still dwelt in them. The dates told her only too clearly that they were all statues of the dead.

The floor of the great hall was of ornamented tile. Walking across it, Judy judged it to be all of a hundred feet wide, and yet she had heard the guide telling the children something about the hall being too small. Too small for what?

She tried to imagine it as it must have been when there were chairs in a semicircle around the room in-

stead of statues. Representatives from every state in
the Union would need seats. Senators, too, on joint session days. And that tiny gallery really was too small
for visitors. Newspaper reporters, too, would need
room.

"I guess they did need a bigger hall," Judy decided.
And yet, as she crossed the tiled floor, the people on the
other side of the room were so far away she could
scarcely hear them talking. It seemed that everyone
had someone to talk with except herself. She wished
Rosita could have come with her instead of hurrying
off with her class.

A group of three men entered the hall. Judy suddenly recognized one of them. He was the nervous
young man who had registered at the motel. Now she
heard a fourth man call out to him, "Hey, Charlie!
Wait right there. I'll be back with the kid."

Charlie waited with the others right under the most
beautiful clock Judy had ever seen. A draped figure
with a tablet in her hands stood in a winged chariot.
The chariot wheel told the time.

"A quarter past nine," Judy whispered.

She had missed the second tour. Tours left every ten
minutes from nine o'clock until about four in the afternoon, she had been told. They took thirty-five minutes.
She could join the third or the fourth tour and still be at
the Department of Justice Building in time to meet
Peter.

"I'll have to tell him about all these statues," she thought, stopping at each one to read what it said on the pedestal.

One immense statue held a scroll bearing the words, *Soul Liberty*. Judy did remember her history well enough to know it was a statue of Roger Williams. He had been banished into the wilderness where he must have felt as alone as she did here in this wilderness of statues.

"Why do they fascinate me so?" she wondered.

Peter had said something about statues being symbolic of the values these men stood for. There was Daniel Webster, for instance. She had seen a movie that pictured his soul as a great white butterfly, symbolic, she supposed, of the greatness of the man. There were no statues of the living. She had discovered that. Even the obscure names like John Gorrie and Uriah M. Rose turned out to be the names of people who had lived and died and been honored by their states.

Judy had heard her father speak of Dr. Gorrie, whose invention of an ice machine to reduce fevers had inspired the modern refrigerator. But she couldn't remember a thing about Uriah M. Rose. It seemed sad, somehow. The statues were beginning to make Judy feel a little creepy. She turned, nearly bumping into a protruding marble foot. The one statue of a woman among all those honored men seemed to stare down at her, disapproving of her clumsy behavior.

*She was alone among the statues when suddenly
the unbelievable happened*

Frances E. Willard, Judy read on her pedestal. She was one of Mrs. Bolton's heroines. Judy's mother was still active in the W. C. T. U., which had been founded by Mrs. Willard. It occurred to Judy that she ought to be active in something instead of wandering around feeling lonely. After school, when she found out where Blackberry was, she could at least contribute a cat to the cause of freedom and democracy.

"Poor Blackberry!" she thought and then checked herself. If he had been taken to a restaurant there was no use wasting sympathy on him. He might like it better than living in the Capitol where so many feet tramping back and forth might disturb his cat naps. Probably he would hide somewhere during the day. But at night when everything was quiet except for the small noises of mice, he would be in his element. Just thinking about it made Judy shiver.

She glanced at the chariot clock once more. Ten minutes had passed. Apparently the three men had become tired of waiting under the clock for the fourth member of the group. They were walking around on the opposite side of the hall looking at statues and talking in low tones. Their voices blended into the murmur of other voices as a few more tourists entered.

On Judy's side of the hall everything was quiet. Too quiet, she was thinking. She was alone among the statues when suddenly the unbelievable happened. A loud whisper sounded in her ear!

CHAPTER VII

The Smiling Senator

WHAT Judy heard was only part of a sentence mentioning Senator Hockett's name. "When he says Soul Liberty . . ." came in a distinct whisper that sounded like a threat. Judy stared at the nearest statue. It hadn't spoken. Common sense told her that much. And yet she had heard the smiling senator's name and the five words that followed exactly as if they had been whispered in her ear.

What could have happened? Judy told herself she must use her head as her father always used to advise her. If she heard a whisper, there had to be someone whispering. Someone alive. Not a statue!

The people on the other side of the room were still talking, their voices only a murmur. "I couldn't have heard a scrap of their conversation," Judy told herself with a shiver that seemed to creep through her veins and give wings to her feet.

Another guided tour was just entering Statuary Hall when Judy fled with the feeling that the place must be haunted. Maybe Peter could explain what had happened. Whatever it was, Judy had no intention of scaring herself further by wandering around through the Capitol Building alone. She was about to pay her quarter and join the next tour when she looked out toward the parking area and saw the sign she had failed to notice before: RESERVED FOR SENATORS ONLY.

"Oh dear!" she exclaimed to the man collecting the quarters. "I'll have to move my car. Will the tour wait?"

"There will be another one in ten minutes."

"Thank you. I may take it."

Everything was suddenly going wrong. Judy might get a ticket for parking in a senator's place and have to pay a fine. Funny, Peter hadn't seen the sign when he left the Beetle there. A door, flanked by the tall columns that made the Capitol Building such an imposing structure, led directly to the semicircular parking field.

A gray-haired man had just finished parking his expensive automobile beside the Beetle. He looked as if he might be a senator or a congressman. Another group of dignified gentlemen were walking toward an elevator that was also reserved for senators.

"Everything is reserved. Where will I park?" Judy wondered as she hurried out to the car, intending to move it. A voice stopped her.

"Leave it there if you like," the voice said kindly. "That's my spot, but I'm not using my car today." Judy whirled around to face the speaker. His voice had startled her. But it was a pleasant voice with no undercurrent of hate in it. There had been hate in that voice that seemed to come from the statue. This voice was all kindness. The man's wide smile and horn-rimmed glasses told Judy at once who he was.

"Senator Hockett!" she exclaimed. "How nice of you to let me park here. I was coming up to your office later. I have a cat I'll be glad to lend you. We called him your catstituent. His name is Blackberry."

The senator's smile widened.

"And yours?"

Judy introduced herself and then, without thinking of the consequences, asked, "Are you planning to make a speech about Soul Liberty?"

The smile vanished from Senator Hockett's face. He looked, for a moment, as if someone had struck him. Then he said, as calmly as if the question had been expected, "I do plan to mention Roger Williams and his influence on our own Declaration of Independence when I introduce a bill my committee now has under consideration. The phrase you mention is somewhere in the speech, but I haven't released it. I don't see how you could have known it unless you are able to read my mind."

Judy could hardly tell him that a statue had whispered the words to her. She smiled and tried to explain some of the things that puzzled her. First there were those voices in the passageway back of the laundry.

"Oh, yes, our room and a couple of the other rooms where tourists are staying back up against that passageway," she said, and added, "My husband came here for a refresher course in the FBI Academy. He's showing me through the Federal Building this afternoon."

"What about this morning? Would you like to visit the Senate?" asked the senator.

"Do you mean it?" exclaimed Judy. "I'd simply love to visit the Senate and the House of Representatives, too. But don't I need a pass or something?"

Senator Hockett was quiet for a moment, as if this were something he hadn't considered. His blue eyes, behind those owlish glasses, were twinkling as he said, "I think that can be arranged. But first let me hear a little bit more about the strange goings-on in this motel where you and your husband are staying."

Judy told him as much as she could remember.

"If you're investigating crime, I thought—I mean if these people who own the motel really have been threatened and forced to pay protection, I thought you might like to know about it," she finished.

"I do, indeed!" Senator Hockett thanked Judy for the information she had given him and said he'd keep in touch. "Now, about the cat?" He had been serious while he was listening to Judy's story, but he was once more a smiling senator as he asked, "Is he a good mouser?"

"Oh, yes," replied Judy. "He hunts mice anywhere. He's used to hunting in our barn at home, but if there are mice in the basement of the Capitol, I'm sure he'll find them."

"They won't be hard to find," Senator Hockett said with a chuckle. "My secretary had quite a scare the last time she went down to get her hair done. It was a 'scare-do' all right. I presume you read that squib in the paper. You aren't the first one to offer me a cat. When can you bring him?"

Judy wished she knew when. She didn't have the note, but she remembered enough of what was in it to tell the senator that she and Peter hoped Blackberry might lead them to the man who was making trouble for Mr. Rocklin.

"He thinks we're working for the—the syndicate or whatever they call themselves. We'll just let him keep on thinking that. You see, Senator Hockett, there's just one difficulty," Judy finished with a little break in her voice, "we have to find Blackberry before we can bring him to you."

"Do you have any idea where to look?"

"A vague one. I met Mr. Rocklin's daughter just a few minutes ago. She was on the tour with her class, but she stopped long enough to tell me the cat had been taken to a restaurant owned by the man who makes the collections."

"In that case, he should be easy to locate."

"That's what I thought," agreed Judy, "but sometimes these things that seem easy turn out to be the hardest of all."

"Now that's a sage remark. May I quote it in one of my speeches?"

Judy consented, not at all sure that Senator Hockett was serious. He kept looking at her as if he expected, her to say something more. He must be wondering how she knew part of a speech he had not yet delivered. Should she explain? *Could* she? There seemed to be no logical explanation for what had happened.

"I'm as puzzled as you are about some of the things I've been telling you," she confessed. "Your speech, for instance. Unless those statues in Statuary Hall can transmit messages—"

"Ah! So that's it," Senator Hockett interrupted before Judy could finish the thought.

"Do you understand it?" she asked in amazement. "I'm sure I don't."

"Wasn't it explained when you took the tour?"

"I didn't—" Judy began, but again she was interrupted. The senator was in a hurry, she could see that.

Already she had taken too much of his valuable time.

"It may be a simple matter of acoustics," he was saying, not making it sound very simple. "Did you notice anybody on the opposite side of the room when you heard the whisper?"

"There were several people all the way across the floor, but I couldn't hear what they were saying," replied Judy, still puzzled. "I was alone on my side of the room. I mean I was alone except for the statues."

"Can you describe these people across the floor?"

"Not all of them. I hardly noticed the tourists, but there were three men whom I've seen at the motel. One of them is called Charlie. You don't think he threw his voice on purpose to frighten me, do you?" Judy asked.

Senator Hockett shook his head, still smiling. He said he was convinced that was not the intention. "*I* am the one who is supposed to be frightened, but don't worry your pretty head about it," he advised Judy just before they parted. "It will take more than a whispered watchword to make me forget my responsibility to the people of America."

CHAPTER VIII

A Forgotten Wish

"So THAT's what it was—a whispered watchword," Judy whispered to herself. Senator Hockett's strange explanation continued to puzzle her. What serious thoughts had he been hiding behind that perpetual smile? Judy wished she knew. They had talked for only a few more minutes before they parted. Blackberry, it was agreed, would be the official mouse-catcher for the Old Senate Office Building as soon as Judy found him. Not only that, but Senator Hockett had presented her with two tickets for Congress.

"Your problems," he had said in parting, "are the problems of the government."

Judy was deeply impressed. She had never thought of it that way before. She gazed long and thoughtfully at the two tickets. One card was orange and the other pale yellow. An eagle with spread wings on the orange card waved the words, VISITOR'S PASS, from a banner in its beak, while its claws clutched an American flag. To the right of the eagle was a picture of the Capitol in a frame of swirls and decorations. This card, previously signed by one of the elected representatives from Pennsylvania, would admit Judy to the House of Representatives. She turned it over and read the rules for visitors.

No packages, bundles, cameras, suitcases, or brief cases were allowed in the House Galleries. Smoking, applause, reading, taking notes, taking photographs, and even the wearing of hats by men were among the things prohibited.

"And they call this a free country," Judy thought, rebelling against these rules just as she used to rebel against what seemed like unnecessary rules at home or in school.

The same rules, she noticed, were printed on the back of the yellow card. On its face were the words, UNITED STATES SENATE CHAMBER, *Washington, D. C.*, followed by the date and Judy's name, admitting her to the reserved gallery. Below was an identical picture of the Capitol without the frame.

Senator Hockett had signed this card himself in a bold and yet, somehow, a friendly hand. It was a brave hand, too. And that smile that made people call him the smiling senator proved to be a courageous smile. During the forenoon as Judy sat in the senate gallery and heard him speak his mind, she became increasingly aware of his courage.

"Peter, I guess was wrong," she told him when she met him by the fountain at twelve-thirty. "All the great men aren't dead. Quite a few of them are alive and working just as hard for democracy today as Jefferson and Lincoln and all the others did in the past. I didn't understand half of what was said in the Senate, but I could tell the senators believed in the truth of what they were saying. Those who were against the bill they were discussing sounded just as sincere as those who were for it."

"Was it Senator Hockett's bill?" asked Peter.

"No, he hasn't introduced his bill yet. I want to be there when he does. This was a bill providing that no memorial be placed on government property here in Washington until fifty years after the death of the person to be honored. I'm in favor of it," declared Judy. "The bill was introduced by a senator from Arizona who keeps harping on it, according to his opponents. I guess this is the fifth or sixth time they've voted it down. This senator says the Capitol is filled with lofty statues of obscure governors and generals, while others more deserving have no monument except the lives they lived."

"That would be monument enough for me," Peter

commented when he could get in a word for himself. "There's a bronze plaque upstairs in the Director's office with the names of Special Agents who have died in the line of duty. It's a great honor, of course, but I prefer to be counted among the living, so let's enjoy the sights here in Washington while we have the chance."

"I'm enjoying them. Did I tell you I met Senator Hockett personally and had a long talk with him?" asked Judy. "He was interested in everything I had to tell him about Blackberry and the motel and everything. Imagine a senator paying that much attention to little me!"

Peter smiled. "You're not so little, Angel. You're taller than your mother. You'll have to write to her this evening and tell her you met her favorite senator."

"He's Dad's favorite, too. And Horace is always quoting him. I'll tell them I saw the Vice President. I couldn't see much more than the top of his head," confessed Judy, "but I knew it was the Vice President because he was sitting in a carved marble chair. There were busts of former Vice Presidents all around the gallery where I was sitting."

"Did they scare you?" Peter asked jokingly.

"Not at all," was Judy's quick retort. "I'm getting used to seeing statues. There's a whole room full of them in what used to be the House of Representatives. It isn't any more, and I can understand why. If that hall isn't haunted it certainly gave a good imitation of it. Senator Hockett says it's the acoustics, whatever that means. I'm going to find out for myself when I use my orange pass."

Peter gave her a puzzled look. "Your orange pass?"

"Yes, for the House of Representatives. I mean the new House. You have to walk through Statuary Hall to get there. That is, if you use the same steps the British used when they sneaked in to burn the Capitol back in 1814. I learned that much just overhearing part of what the guide said when she was conducting a tour. And Peter, do you know who was taking that tour? Rosita! She was touring with her class, but I managed to pull her aside and have a few words with her."

"A few words!" exclaimed Peter when Judy stopped for breath. "Is that possible?"

Judy had been talking constantly ever since she arrived at their meeting place. That was one of the wonderful things about Peter. He really listened when she talked. He wasn't always preoccupied with what he wanted to say himself the way a lot of people were. His blue eyes widened as she continued.

"Rosita says Blackberry was taken to a restaurant. She's going to tell me where the restaurant is after she's talked with her father. She would have told me this morning only she couldn't remember the name."

"Speaking of restaurants, don't you think we ought to be looking for one? Let's go," Peter suggested.

"It's so peaceful here by the fountain. I almost dread going into a noisy restaurant," confessed Judy. "I walked all around this building before I remembered that you said the fountain was *inside*. You might call it a hidden fountain."

From the outside, as they looked back at it, the Department of Justice Building appeared much like all the other buildings on Pennsylvania Avenue. Judy had passed the U. S. Court House, a library and the National Archives Building when she walked over from the Capitol.

"I was tempted to go in and see the Declaration of Independence," she confessed, "but there wasn't time. Besides, I want you to be with me when I see it."

"Suppose we see it now, during our lunch hour," Peter suggested.

A few minutes later Judy was gazing through glass at the famous document and Peter was telling her how it had been treated with chemicals to preserve the original writing. The guard who stood there guiding the line of tourists, most of them students, seemed proud of his job.

"He could be a minister," Judy whispered, "and we could be in church."

There wasn't time to see the other documents under glass along the walls. Old Colonial charters, the Constitution, the Bill of Rights, and many more of the most valued government papers were kept there, and Judy wanted to stay and really look at them. After such food for the spirit, lunch seemed unimportant to her.

Lunch was never unimportant to Peter. While they were eating at a restaurant just across Pennsylvania Avenue from the two famous buildings, he told Judy more about old documents.

"Their age can be determined in the FBI laboratory," he explained. "The Dead Sea Scrolls were taken there and examined. They were hidden in a cave for two thousand years where no sunlight could reach them."

"Did the darkness preserve them?" asked Judy.

"The darkness and the cool air." Peter picked up his glass, finished the milk in it and then looked at it closely. "They were kept in jars, I believe. Anyway, it was quite a discovery. I guess the goatherd who found them had no idea he had discovered anything so ancient."

"It makes a person wonder, doesn't it?" agreed Judy. "We've made a few discoveries ourselves, but nothing that important. I wish—"

"Save it and wish in the fountain just before you start on the tour," advised Peter. "I'll give you a coin to toss in for luck."

"My wish wouldn't be worth it. I've forgotten what I started to wish, anyway," confessed Judy. "Maybe it had something to do with these passes Senator Hockett gave me. They're good for the entire Congress except on joint session days." Judy held them out for Peter's inspection. "It says that on the back. See, where all the rules are printed. Peter, why do there have to be so many rules?"

"You'll see why before the afternoon is over," he told her. "The FBI tour is all arranged. It should take about two hours."

CHAPTER IX

More Wishes

Judy finished her dessert quickly. Soon she and Peter were ready to leave the restaurant. "One restaurant crossed off our list," Judy was thinking. Blackberry might be found in any one of a thousand others.

As they were crossing the street, Peter pointed out something odd about the Archives Building. It had no windows, only those tall columns Judy had seen on so many of the buildings in Washington. Next to it the Department of Justice Building waited to be toured. She had looked forward to the tour for so long that she felt a little shiver of excitement as they entered.

When they were inside standing beside the fountain Peter handed Judy a coin. "Here you are. Now make your wish," he said half seriously.

Other coins had been tossed in the water. Other wishes had been made. Had they come true? Again Judy found herself wondering.

"How can I wish? What I really want isn't for myself, anyway," she confided. "It's all tied in with the things I want for other people, too. Rosita, for instance. I might wish she didn't have to be watched every minute as if she were a criminal. And, of course, there's Blackberry. I wish we'd find him."

"That's a wish worth making," declared Peter. "We *must* find the old fellow, though I don't suppose he's pining away for us if he's living in a restaurant and eating plenty of fish."

"You're just trying to make me feel better," charged Judy, "but it won't work. I'd rather have him living in the basement of the Capitol catching mice."

"I can see you're eager to take him there. Why don't you wish him back in our room waiting for us when we return to the motel?" Peter suggested.

Judy felt it was an impossible wish. She wouldn't have tossed her coin in the fountain if some of the students waiting to take the tour hadn't been making wishes and laughing about them. Judy laughed, too, but inside she felt like crying. Blackberry wouldn't be there no matter how hard she wished.

"Peter, can't we do something practical to make my wish come true?" she asked as the coin sank to the bottom of the pool around the fountain. "You said you'd put an ad in the paper."

"It's in," he replied, "but it won't appear until tomorrow morning. There's nothing we can do about it today until Rosita gives us the name of that restaurant she mentioned. In the meantime, there is something I want to show you. We were talking about ancient documents before. Well, our Document Section handles everything from fraudulent checks to old love letters . . ."

Judy couldn't help thinking of a pack of old love letters she had discovered in the attic when the Bolton family first moved to Farringdon. They were found to be letters from Peter's mother to his father. Brought up by his grandparents, he had known very little about his parents or his baby sister before the letters were discovered. Afterwards . . . but that was another mystery, solved when Judy was not quite sixteen.

"I was thinking about some old love letters that were pretty important to us," she explained when Peter caught her gazing into the fountain and daydreaming. "Remember how they mentioned Baby G— and that was all we could make out because the mice in our attic had made a feast of them."

"Afterwards, Blackberry made a feast of the mice," Peter recalled, thinking back with Judy. "I do keep forgetting Honey's real name is Grace. It was your brother Horace who first spoke to her."

"I wish he'd speak to her again," declared Judy. "Wouldn't it be wonderful if they'd get married and come to Washington on their honeymoon?"

"A honeymoon for Honey," joked Peter. "Don't wish for it just yet. They have lots of time. Horace doesn't rush into things the way you do, and Honey isn't ready to leave Grandpa and Grandma. Ever since those old love letters and your clever detective work changed things for her, she's felt she had to make up to them for all the loving they'd missed."

"I know," agreed Judy. "Those letters brought us closer together, too. Remember when you said, 'Some day you'll be writing love letters of your own'? But when I did write them they were all to you, Peter. I guess I wrote to you almost every day when you were away studying law in New York and Honey was going to art school."

"I guess you've forgotten most of those letters were to Honey. You fell in love with somebody else about then," Peter reminded her.

"If you're thinking of Arthur Farringdon-Pett, it didn't last long and I did keep on writing. Right now," Judy said, deliberately changing the subject, "there's another letter I'd like to discuss. It's that message from Mr. Rocklin. Did you find out anything more?"

"Not yet," replied Peter. "It will be examined under ultra violet light in our Document Section. I thought you might like to watch."

Judy knew the FBI Laboratory was divided into a number of different sections and units. She wanted to tour every one of them. She turned to say something of the kind to Peter, but he was no longer beside her.

When he returned he was with another FBI agent. He was speaking to the whole group, not just to Judy, when he announced that a guided tour was forming at the Ninth Street and Pennsylvania Avenue entrance.

"But that's the regular tour," Judy protested, following him along with five or six others who had been waiting at the fountain for the tour to begin. Judy had expected her tour to be a little special.

At the entrance another group waited. Peter introduced himself and then turned to speak privately with the other agent whose name, appropriately, turned out to be Mr. Gunn. Both agents wore their pictures on ribbons around their necks as if they were lockets. Peter's picture didn't do him justice, Judy thought. His sandy hair looked black in the photograph, and his blue eyes appeared gray.

"Aren't you going to show me through the laboratory yourself?" Judy asked him in surprise when Mr. Gunn continued the speech Peter had begun.

"Not this time, Angel," Peter replied. "Something has come up. You may see me in the Document Section."

"Is it about the note?"

But Peter had gone, leaving Judy's question unanswered. Wondering, she and the others taking the tour followed Mr. Gunn.

He did not take them at once to the Document Section. Under a large sign that said FEDERAL BUREAU OF INVESTIGATION, *Identification Unit*, everybody stopped to look at the nine types of fingerprint patterns displayed.

As Judy studied the different types of fingerprints her thoughts returned to Honey. They were now sisters as well as chums. But none of the experiences they had shared would have been possible if it hadn't been for a tiny heart-shaped thumb print that did not seem to fit immediately into any of the patterns.

"In our files are over one hundred and fifty million sets of fingerprints," Mr. Gunn was saying. "Since fingerprints are the only known means of positive identification, the value of this collection is beyond calculation. A thousand or more wanted criminals are identified monthly. Our files also contain many tales of broken family circles which have been mended through the assistance of fingerprint records."

Peter's broken family circle had been one of those mended, thought Judy. She wished he were there to explain things himself. She wanted to ask him about Honey's thumb print. It had been the means of reuniting Peter's sister with the family she hadn't even known she had. Mr. Gunn's explanation of the importance of fingerprint identification was lost on Judy. She already knew!

A little later, standing around a desk, Judy and the

others were amazed to see what Mr. Gunn called a latent fingerprint being reconstructed by means of lines that looked to her like the rays of the sun. She was reminded of the way the streets of Washington slanted. A fleeting thought came to her. "Where will I meet Peter if I don't find him in the Document Section? Will I know the way back to the motel without him?" He had said he would be using an official car. The Beetle would be hers. It was still parked in Senator Hockett's place just east of the Capitol Building.

Deliberately Judy turned her thoughts back to the pencilled lines that were being used to reconstruct a clear fingerprint.

"This print was taken from a glass paperweight," Mr. Gunn was explaining to the tourists grouped around the desk.

"A glass paperweight!" The words hit Judy. The exclamation was involuntary. "Why, that looks like the paperweight we found—"

She stopped, realizing this was something she wasn't free to tell. Peter had meant to show her that paperweight. Judy knew it. Without him she was just another tourist as alone as she had been among those statues in the Capitol.

"I wish I knew who really whispered that threat to Senator Hockett," she thought.

CHAPTER X

Liz Holbrook

IT HAD been a threat. Suddenly Judy was sure of it. Peter ought to know about it. Judy tried to remember just what she had told him. She had mentioned the word *acoustics* and said something about Statuary Hall being haunted. That was all. It wasn't enough to make Peter realize the seriousness of what she had heard. She hadn't realized herself that it was anything urgent at first. But now as she followed the tour past a row of glassed-in cubicles where trained technicians designed and developed electronic equipment, she began to wonder.

"I am the one who is supposed to be frightened," Senator Hockett had said.

He seemed to think the mysterious whisper had carried, somehow, clear across Statuary Hall. If she had taken the guided tour it would have been explained. Probably it had been explained to some of the students walking beside her. They would have toured the Capitol Building before taking the FBI tour. She was about to ask one of them when a voice spoke at her elbow.

"You're Mrs. Peter Dobbs, aren't you?"

Startled out of her thoughts, Judy did not answer immediately. It was obvious who she was as she had been seen with Peter when he was wearing his identification around his neck. She smiled at the speaker, a fair-haired girl of possibly seventeen or eighteen. She had taken her to be one of the group of students, but now she realized her mistake.

"Haven't I seen you somewhere before?" Judy asked.

"Probably," was the amused reply. "I've been walking right beside you ever since you made your wish in the fountain. I wished something, too. I wished you and I would get to know each other better. I'm Liz Holbrook. You're staying at the Eagle Motel, aren't you?"

Judy laughed. "I guess that's its name. There are eagles all over the place. Now I know where I saw you. Weren't you at the switchboard yesterday?"

"I was. Today's my day off," Liz explained. "I

thought I'd see the sights. What about you?"

"The same," replied Judy, feeling a little less lonely now that she had someone to talk with. "Seeing the sights and learning as much as I can. I keep bumping into people from the motel. First there was Mr. Rocklin's daughter touring the Capitol with her class, and then a man I recognized, and now you."

"Who was the man? Maybe I know him."

Judy described him as well as she could.

"I noticed his eyes when he registered," she explained. "He registered for a whole group of people. We have the room next to the suite he rented. He said it was a business conference. We could hear them talking through the walls."

"Is that why your husband took that particular room?" Liz asked.

The question came so abruptly that it surprised Judy. Suddenly she realized that Peter could have rented the outside room instead of the inside one she wanted for that very reason. He didn't always tell her his motives. "His work is confidential," she said. "He isn't allowed to discuss it."

"That's too bad," Liz said, "because there's something I have to discuss with someone. Have you met Mr. Rocklin, the motel manager?"

"No," Judy replied guardedly, "but I've talked with his daughter."

"You talked with Rosita?" Liz sounded surprised.

"It was only for a few minutes," Judy explained. "Then she hurried on with her class. The teacher had her hands full keeping watch of so many children. I guess they were having a final outing before school lets out for the summer. Rosita seemed to be enjoying it. Poor girl! She deserves a little freedom. Mrs. Rocklin won't let her out of her sight."

"Her father dotes on her, too," Liz agreed with a sidewise glance at Judy. "He'd never forgive himself if anything happened to her."

"He's afraid something will. They're both terribly afraid. Do you know why?" Judy asked hopefully.

Liz laughed. "Maybe it's that cat someone left in the motel. Some people say a black cat is a forewarning of evil."

"This one isn't. He's my cat, and I didn't leave him in the room to frighten people," Judy protested. "I brought him from home. I've taken him on lots of trips and he never—" She stopped herself and said truthfully, "I mean he seldom made trouble. Anyway, I didn't plant him. Mr. Rocklin thought I did. He left a note saying he had given the cat back to someone. Do you know who has him now?"

Liz shook her head. "I haven't any idea."

"Rosita said it was a man who owns a restaurant. I thought you might know his name."

"There are plenty of men who own restaurants."

"I know." Judy would have said more, but just then

Liz caught sight of a phone booth and remembered a call she had to make. When she rejoined the tour they were in the Document Section, but there was no sign of Peter.

Her mind on the problems of the Rocklin family, Judy gazed at samples of extortion notes and vicious threats made by kidnappers. She heard something about sixteen thousand fraudulent checks, sixty-two thousand signatures, and a printer who had conceived the bright idea of printing his own checks and cashing them. So many charges had piled up against him that his sentences totaled a hundred and fifty years.

"That's more than a lifetime. Think of spending your whole life in prison!" exclaimed one of the students taking the tour.

"I'd rather not think of it." Liz shrugged her shoulders, affecting a sophisticated air of indifference. It was hard for Judy to decide whether or not she liked her. She found herself answering questions instead of asking them.

"This tour would have been more interesting if your husband could have been our guide. Where do you suppose he is?" Liz asked as they left the Document Section. "You were supposed to meet him here, weren't you?"

"He said he might be here. I guess you heard him. He may be waiting for me in the Director's office," she added.

The director, she soon learned, was out of town. The tour took in only his outer office where Judy and the others were introduced to one of his assistants and listened to an account of the Bureau's early beginnings.

"You'll see it all in pictures," the assistant finished, waving his hand toward a rack of cartoons that had appeared in newspapers through the years. One cartoon showed the FBI as an eye in the sky watching a gang of hoodlums. Another screamed the headlines: FBI DOES IT AGAIN. One of the ten most wanted men had been captured, and the cartoon showed another criminal being moved in to take his place.

"That's the way it goes," Liz said, walking over to stand beside Judy. "It's always the FBI. Individual agents are seldom given credit."

"That's the way it should be," Judy retorted, quick to defend the Bureau's position. "The FBI has to keep its agents as anonymous as possible."

"Anonymous is right. Their lives aren't really their own. But you'll get used to disappointments and take them in your stride the way I do. My husband is a G-man, too."

This announcement surprised Judy so much that it was a moment before she could find her voice. Could it be true? It would be pleasant to know another young FBI wife like herself. Liz appeared to be even younger than Judy, and she did live at the same motel. Was she working at the switchboard in order to report what she heard? It was an interesting possibility. "Surprised?" asked Liz. "You didn't think we had so much in common, did you?" "Bewildered is a better word," declared Judy. "I have to readjust my thinking. Did we just happen to meet, or was this something our husbands planned?" "They may have planned it," Liz admitted. "My Charlie works right here in the building. He's in one of the laboratories. I'll introduce him to you if we happen to see him."

"That will be nice," agreed Judy, still a little dazed by Liz Holbrook's revelation.

The others taking the tour had hurried ahead with Mr. Gunn, like sheep following their leader. They were on their way to the serology laboratory where blood stains were analyzed.

"We sent a sheet here once. It was worn by someone playing ghost along what we called the haunted road. It gives me the shivers just to think of it," confessed Judy. "I'm glad they aren't going to analyze my blood. I'm sure it must be running cold."

"Mine, too," agreed Liz. "Let's not go with them. Let's do a little exploring by ourselves. I'd like to find Charlie. Wouldn't you?"

Judy was tempted. After all, she had planned this tour with Peter. There was no reason why she and Liz should be treated like ordinary tourists and kept out of the laboratories. Afterwards she wasn't sure which one of them opened the door. They were greeted by a white-coated young man who inquired courteously, "May I help you?"

"Oh, I beg your pardon," Liz said. "I thought my husband would be in here. This is another FBI wife, Mrs. Peter Dobbs."

"I know Peter—"

"I thought you would," Judy interrupted eagerly. "I've heard about the work of the spectograph," she continued, recognizing the instrument from Peter's description. "It makes little rainbows, doesn't it? May we see it in operation?"

"You may." The young man hesitated, obviously annoyed. He was examining pigments of paint taken from the fender of a wrecked car. The examination would determine what had hit it, he explained, pointing out a rack of automobile paints.

"Do you compare colors? Is that how the rainbow machine gives you the answers?" asked Liz.

"Please!" he corrected her in a pained voice. "These are delicate scientific instruments, not machines. Are you on a special tour?"

"Very special," Liz answered mischievously.

CHAPTER XI

An Alarming Thought

The scientific instruments in the room were delicate. Judy looked at Liz. They had been calling each other by first names and feeling very chummy. But now, suddenly, there was a barrier between them.

"We aren't really on a special tour," Judy said honestly to the young man. "We ought not to have come in here without permission. We'll leave right away."

"We will in a minute." Liz had made a quick motion with her hand as she spoke. Something clattered to the floor. Judy didn't see what it was.

"Come on," she urged, "before you break something. Maybe we can overtake the tour before Mr. Gunn misses us. I don't want to get Peter in trouble with the Bureau."

"Does it matter?" Liz asked. "He could go into private practice. There's more money in it."

"Not always." Judy was remembering Peter's little law office in Roulsville where she had first worked as his secretary. It had been a struggle. If Peter had been willing to work for the racketeers he would have been well paid. Instead, he had made a reputation for honesty in all his dealings. He had been investigated, as all prospective FBI agents are, and found to qualify. Not for anything would Judy hurt his reputation.

"The Bureau wouldn't approve of what we've done. I'm always doing reckless things and regretting it," confessed Judy. "Once I almost became a target for one of Peter's bullets because I rushed ahead trying to solve a mystery before he did."

Liz smiled as if she suddenly saw the light. "So that's how it is? You're really in competition with him. I thought you must have an angle."

"No, you have it all wrong. It isn't that way at all." Judy tried to explain, but it was no use.

"You can't fool me," Liz declared. "Oh, I know you don't want to get Peter in trouble. You just want to be there a little ahead of him."

"Where?" asked Judy.

Liz shrugged her shoulders in that characteristic gesture. "You tell me. I don't know where he is."

"I'm not looking for him," Judy retorted. "That was your idea. I'm looking for Mr. Gunn. Whether we like it or not, he's our official guide."

"Well, let's find him then," Liz suggested. "Shall we take the elevator or walk?"

Judy thought it would be better to take the elevator. After all, there were eight stories to the Department of Justice Building and the tour might be on any one of them. She inquired of the elevator operator and found out exactly where Mr. Gunn and his followers were.

Arriving at one of the lower floors, Liz hurried up to their official guide and made some sort of an apology.

"I didn't think the rules applied to the wives of Special Agents," she ended her excuse.

"They certainly do," was the sharp reply.

A little later Mr. Gunn took Judy aside and gave her a short lecture on the duties of FBI wives while Liz stood listening as if the talk interested her hardly at all. He gave Judy a pamphlet issued by the United States Department of Justice entitled: WHAT IT'S LIKE TO BE AN FBI AGENT. It described Clarence Wilton, not his real name, of course. He was the typical G-man and Mrs. Wilton, obviously, was the perfect wife.

"Their comfortable house is decorated with oils painted by Mrs. Wilton, and as often as possible, with vases of her husband's favorite flower, roses," Liz read aloud from the pamphlet. Turning to Judy, she asked, "What's Peter's favorite flower?"

"I'm afraid I don't know," confessed Judy, her mind on the lecture Mr. Gunn had given her. He had reminded her that Peter, as a field man, was on call twenty-four hours a day.

"He is *never* off duty," Mr. Gunn had reminded her soberly. "Every three hours during the day, from wherever he is working, he must call the office for messages and new assignments. At night, if he goes to a movie, he must tell his office the telephone number of the theater. One lead on the whereabouts of a wanted criminal is apt to send him off on another. You must not expect him to keep appointments or hold him to his promises," he had finished the lecture. "As his wife, you must not try to find out anything about his assignments."

"In other words," Liz said, summing it all up for Judy as the tour continued, "the good little FBI wife can't possibly make a hobby of solving mysteries."

"No," Judy admitted with a sigh, "I'm afraid she can't. She has to find some other hobby such as oil painting or flower arranging. Cooking is all right, I guess, if her husband is ever there to eat the stuff she cooks."

"She has to be a good homemaker, but what sort of a home can she make if she has to follow her husband from one assignment to another?" Liz continued their joint complaint.

"She doesn't always follow him around," Judy put in. "Sometimes he is a resident agent. Then she can have a real home."

"Like yours?" Liz questioned.

"I do have a house, but it's rented for the summer. It was my grandmother's home," Judy explained. "She left it to me hoping we'd have a family some day. I hope we will, too, but right now I want to be able to travel with Peter."

Judy remembered Peter's promise that they would be a team. He had told her the trip she had taken to . Yellowstone National Park would be her last long trip without him. Instead of Peter, his sister Honey had accompanied her. Together they had solved one of the strangest mysteries Judy had ever encountered.

"If the government doesn't pin a medal on you for what you've done, I will," Peter had told her.

She had hoped to meet the Director and receive, at least, a word of commendation. Instead, she had met his assistant as one of a group on a conducted tour. And it wasn't a medal but a scolding she had received. Everything she had done was wrong.

Judy looked at her new friend, wondering what she was really like underneath that mask of indifference she seemed to be wearing.

"What about you?" Judy questioned. "Did Mr. Gunn's lecture upset any of your plans?"

"Not at all," Liz replied. "It strengthened them, if anything. I'm going to talk Charlie out of the work he's doing while there's still time. I have other plans for him. Lots of other plans!"

Judy didn't like the way Liz said that. Loyalty to Peter's work was one of the first things she herself had learned as a bride. It had been just the other way around with them. She had practically talked Peter into government work. It had meant long separations, hours of anxiety, but always pride in him when his work was finished.

"I see it as a service to my country," he had once told her.

Ignoring Liz who, apparently, did not see it that way at all, Judy moved closer to hear what Mr. Gunn was saying. His lecture on the special exhibits they had been viewing was ended. Judy vowed she would see them again with Peter and really listen.

"And now," Mr. Gunn continued as they moved on, "we come to an extremely important work of the Bureau—National Security."

He pointed out a display of bolts, coins, pencils, and a number of other things in which microfilm had been hidden. Periods, magnified, were shown to be micro-dots. A map or a secret message could be concealed in a dot no bigger than the head of a pin.

"Our agents were instructed to look for dots. The magnifying glass in the display case shows you what they found," Mr. Gunn finished as he led the group to an exhibit of firearms.

Judy had never liked guns of any description. Peter carried the Colt .38 special issued by the Bureau, but

he was trained to use other types. In the case were
many kinds of weapons all the way from machine guns
down to a tiny pistol concealed in a fountain pen.
These, Judy learned to her horror, were sold by some
mail order houses.

"No wonder Congress has rules against taking notes
in the Senate gallery!" she exclaimed. "If some criminal
who wanted to eliminate a senator . . ."

She did not finish the thought. A swift premonition
came over her. Or was it a premonition? There was
something she had just about figured out when Liz
first spoke to her. Something she had to remember!

"Are you coming?" asked Liz. "We're taking the
elevator to the basement. This is the most exciting part
of the tour. We're going to watch those crack G-men
really shoot."

CHAPTER XII

The Milk Bottle Area

In the basement Judy stood with the others. A screen separated them from a long alley with targets at the end of it. The targets didn't look too much like men. They were divided into sections. Each section was marked with a number.

"It's like a game," Liz remarked, standing so close to Judy that she could hear her breathing. "I guess that's how they score."

Shooting would never be like a game to Judy. It was deadly serious. Peter had recently been wounded in a gun battle. She knew he had come to Washington for a refresher course in the use of firearms. This must be where he practiced. But where was he now? There was so much she wanted to tell him—half completed thoughts that she felt sure he could finish. They darted about in her head, giving rise to new fears.

"I thought maybe you'd find your husband down here practicing," Liz said with a sidelong glance at Judy as Mr. Gunn introduced two strange G-men and announced that they would give a demonstration of the four basic FBI weapons—pistol, submachine gun, shotgun, and rifle.

"You didn't find *your* husband anywhere, did you?" Judy whispered back.

The G-men who were giving the demonstration had turned their backs to take aim at the targets at the end of the alley. The crack of their guns soon shattered the air and sent shivers up and down Judy's spine.

"If those targets were real men, they wouldn't have a chance," declared Liz, and Judy could feel her shivering, too.

The men who were shooting hit the target in what Mr. Gunn called the milk bottle area every time. No twos or threes for the more remote parts of the body were scored. They hit nothing but fives.

"They're good, aren't they?" Judy couldn't help admiring their skill.

Liz gasped. "Do you call that good? They shoot to kill."

"Only when a criminal resists arrest," replied Judy.

Mr. Gunn had just finished telling them that an FBI

agent must be trained to protect his own body by shooting from behind a wall, a tree, or any object that happened to be handy.

"If it's a raid, he shouts his warning and then closes in. Usually the frightened criminal comes out with his

hands up. That's the way it happened when Machine Gun Kelly first named us G-men," Mr. Gunn continued. "When the gangster found his house surrounded by government men he called out in a trembling voice: 'Don't shoot, G-men, don't shoot!' That was in the early thirties when a wave of lawlessness swept over the nation. These men you have just been watching are trained to see that it doesn't happen again."

"It mustn't happen," Judy whispered fiercely.

Suddenly she remembered the wish she had forgot-

ten. It was a wish for Senator Hockett's safety. He intended to make that speech with the words *Soul Liberty* in it in spite of the danger. It was up to Judy to find Peter and tell him. She was sure now that the whisper she had heard hadn't really come from her

side of Statuary Hall at all, but from the other side
where those men were talking and planning!

It was when Judy thought of what they must be
planning that she became really frightened. "When he
says *Soul Liberty* . . ." the voice had whispered and
she had heard the tag end of a sentence ending with
Senator Hockett's name. It was clear now. *Soul Liberty*
must be their watchword. But what would they do
when he said the words? And how did they know they
were in his speech—unless his secretary or someone
working with him had betrayed him?

"The tour is over. I don't think you're going to find
Peter," Liz broke in on Judy's thoughts. "He may be
out shooting at real criminals instead of targets. Or
maybe it's the other way around."

Judy clutched her arm. "Don't talk like that! You
frighten me."

"Think *I'm* not frightened?" Liz returned. "You
were my pal, and all the time I'll bet you knew—"

"Knew *what?*" asked Judy. "I don't know what
you're talking about, and it's what I don't know that
scares me. These guns aren't half as deadly as the ones
upstairs. I mean all those trophies our G-men captured
from criminals. That tiny pistol inside a fountain pen
could kill a man, and yet they're sold by mail order
houses. Anyone can buy them. Senator Hockett thinks
there ought to be a law—"

"There will be if Senator Hockett has his way," Liz

put in, and Judy detected the same note of hate in her voice that she had heard in the whisper.

"What's the matter, Liz?" she asked suspiciously. "If your husband is a laboratory assistant, you don't need to be afraid he's out somewhere shooting at criminals. Or are you really afraid it's the other way around?" she added accusingly.

"You're too smart, Judy," Liz replied in a low voice. "You knew I was lying. You probably know exactly why I'm here."

"I know you've been sticking to me closer than my own shadow," Judy retorted.

"I was following orders, but if you know about the plot against Senator Hockett, and from what you said just now, I'm sure you do—"

"Oh, that?" Judy interrupted, not daring to confess how little she really knew. "The senator trusts me, of course. If you don't believe it, why don't you walk over to the Capitol with me? My car's parked in his space."

"It is? That's dangerous, you know. It could be mistaken for his. Look, Judy, we're pals, aren't we? I did lie to you, but we can still be pals. Isn't that right?"

Judy smiled. "Of course, Liz. If you're in any sort of trouble I'll help you. But we have to be honest with each other, don't we? I really thought your husband was an FBI agent when you first told me. Now I'm not sure what to think. You don't look old enough to have a husband."

"I'm seventeen," Liz said defensively. "I quit high school and got married because my folks kept nagging at me, but it didn't help much. Now Charlie nags. I've been married for two months, I swear it."

"I believe you," Judy said, taking Liz by the hand. "Shall we talk about it while we walk over to the Capitol? I may have met your Charlie. What does he really do?"

"Why, he—he's in business. It's a big organization. He travels a lot," Liz explained. "That's why I got the job at the motel."

Judy didn't see the connection, but it wasn't the time to ask about it. What she did see was more urgent. Liz was really frightened, and she was ready to talk.

"You'll take me back, won't you?" the younger girl pleaded.

"Back where?" asked Judy. Was Liz asking for a ride back to the motel? She hadn't said so.

"Please," she begged, still not making it clear where she wanted to go. "If there was a raid and Charlie got shot in—in the milk bottle area— Oh dear! That's the area around the heart. I guess it would be too late then, wouldn't it?"

"Are you just guessing?" asked Judy. "Oh, I hope Peter hasn't been sent out on a raid. Why do you think such a thing?"

"There are lots of reasons. Charlie's fingerprints could be on that paperweight. He really thought you and Peter were criminals, and now you probably think Charlie is."

"Frankly," Judy admitted, "I don't know what to think. But if Peter's been sent out on a raid, he *may* be shooting at real targets."

"My Charlie could be one of them! I—I hope he got the message I left for him when I called. I had to warn him, Judy. He isn't really bad. He's just afraid of being called chicken. I guess Mom's right. We're both just a couple of mixed-up kids. That's what she says. She's always crying and saying it's her fault because she spoiled me. But it wasn't really. It was my own fault because I always yelled until I got my way."

Liz stopped, out of breath. Judy could feel nothing but sympathy for her even if her Charlie, as she called him, and Peter were on opposite sides of the law. But a raid! Judy hoped Liz's guess was wrong.

"You will take me home, won't you?" Liz persisted. "Charlie dropped me off this morning, and I have no way of getting back to the motel unless you take me. Oh, I could take a bus or a taxi—"

"But you don't want to? All right," agreed Judy. "I'm not very familiar with Washington streets. You can direct me."

CHAPTER XIII

Misdirected

LIZ agreed to her suggestion almost too readily, Judy thought. They were walking along Pennsylvania Avenue toward Capitol Hill as they talked. It was a warm day, but the shade trees made it a pleasant walk. Crossing Constitution Avenue, they soon reached the monument to peace where the curved walk branched off. This was the walk she and Peter had taken. Was it only last night? Judy stopped by one of those mysterious grottos. It was open now. Someone must have removed the cement slab.

"Peter was right. There is a little fountain inside, but there's no water in it," she commented, peering in.

Liz, as usual, was right beside her. She started to say

something and then checked herself. Judy could see she was startled.

"What is it?" she asked. "Did you hear anything strange? I thought I heard something inside this grotto last night. But there's nothing there now."

"That's right," Liz agreed. "There's nothing but an old dry fountain. Charlie said—" Again she stopped. Who was this Charlie, anyway? Had he said something Liz was afraid to tell? Had he *whispered* something, maybe? By now, Judy was fairly certain he was the young man she had seen registering at the motel and later in Statuary Hall.

"How does he sign his name?" Judy asked. "Charles Holbrook?"

"No," Liz denied. "He signs it Charlie Caro. I'm Mrs. Caro. Liz Holbrook is my maiden name. Mom and Dad always called me Betty. I hated it. Betty sounds so babyish. It made me *feel* like a baby, so I named myself Liz."

"Is that what Charlie calls you?"

"Sometimes. Mostly he calls me Chicken. I hate that name, too," Liz confessed in a sudden outburst of emotion. "He's the one who's chicken. He's afraid of losing his job. He does everything his boss tells him. Orders, he says! He takes orders from a cousin who married into the family, too. I trusted *him* once, but not any more. I don't know why I'm telling you all this, but Charlie's father is Mrs. Rocklin's brother. That makes me a sort of cousin by marriage to Rosita, and she's the nicest one in the whole family. If anything happens to her . . ."

"Do you really think she's in danger?" Judy asked when Liz stopped as if she had said too much.

"Oh, I hope not!" she cried. "The teacher shouldn't have taken her on that tour. She didn't know the danger. Let's hurry, Judy. I want to make sure she's all right."

They were approaching the west side of the Capitol Building. Judy thought it was much more beautiful than the east side. There were more trees. Yes, and more statues. She glanced up at the dome topped by the statue of Freedom. There were two smaller domes on either side. The one on the right must be the domed ceiling of Statuary Hall.

"Have you ever toured the Capitol?" she asked Liz.

"Not really," was the evasive answer. "I've been in and out."

"Have you ever been in Statuary Hall?"

"You mean the hall where you hear the whisper? Yes, I've been there, but I didn't stand in the right spot, I guess. I didn't hear anything unusual."

"Well, I did," Judy said. She might as well tell her and find out for sure if Liz's Charlie was the man the others had called "Charlie" just before she heard the whispered watchword. "There were several people on the other side of the hall, and I think one of them was your husband. He must have thrown his voice, or the acoustics in the hall did it. I don't understand it at all, but that's how I know about the plot against Senator Hockett. When he says the words *Soul Liberty*, something is going to happen—",

"Not if I can help it," Liz interrupted.

"You're with me then?"

"All the way," declared Liz, and Judy felt sure she meant it.

They walked through the Capitol to the parking space. The last guided tour had left. The corridors of the building were quiet, echoing their footsteps. They passed the architect's office, the old stone stairway, and another hall where there were several statues of women and a model of the Capitol the way it would be when all the proposed repairs were finished. Workmen were still busy on the east front. New pillars were being put up. The old pillars were now part of the inside wall. Liz looked at the workmen, now ready to leave for their homes.

"I wonder if they have to pay protection," she said.

"Do you think they do? Oh, Liz! Not in the Capitol!" exclaimed Judy.

Liz shook her head. "They're powerful. They're in politics right now. Charlie keeps telling me. He can't get out, he says, and live to talk about it. Well, I'm talking about it, and I'm still alive."

Judy didn't know what to say to that. It sounded

too serious for a quick reply. She'd have to talk it over with Peter. There was so much she had to talk over with him! She did hope he'd be at the motel.

When they reached the car Judy found that the other cars parked beside the Beetle were no longer there. The senators must have all gone home. Except in emergencies she knew that Congress was usually in session only in the morning.

"Tomorrow morning," she decided, "I intend to be back here. I want to be sitting in the gallery when Senator Hockett makes his speech about Soul Liberty. I want to find out what this is all about."

"Don't you *know*, Judy? You're the one who told me what they're planning. They hate Senator Hockett. He's going to wreck the business with that new law."

"Do you mean your husband's business?" Judy asked quietly. It was becoming clear to her now. Liz's Charlie must be in some business that would be hurt if the federal government had more control over it. There was the manufacture of those pistol pens, for instance. Senator Hockett's law would put the manufacturers out of business, and someone would lose money. Was that the key to the whole problem?

"It's an honest business," Liz said as she seated herself beside Judy in the car. "Anyway, it was until they moved in. Charlie's boss didn't hold out the way Rosita's father is doing. He just laughed and said, 'If you can't lick 'em, join 'em.'"

Judy thought that was a bad rule. She had always

thought so. You didn't join a gang of hoodlums just because you couldn't beat them. You didn't go over to the wrong side just because the right side appeared to be losing. She tried to explain this to Liz as she backed the car a few feet, turned, and headed south the way Liz directed her. Soon they were driving down Independence Avenue past all those turreted buildings Judy had seen when she and Peter were standing on the Capitol steps. They were looking west. She knew that.

"Aren't we turned around?" she asked Liz. "The motel is in the northeast section, isn't it?"

"I know. Just drive along here till we get to Twelfth Street. Then turn left and cross the railroad."

"You're sure?"

"Oh, yes," Liz said airily. "I've taken this route home plenty of times. Twelfth runs into Maine. You drive along Maine Avenue by the water until you get to M Street. Then you drive east to Eleventh, and that takes you right into Maryland Avenue. You know the motel's near the corner of New York and Maryland, don't you?"

"If you say so," Judy agreed. "I know it's on New York Avenue not too far past Florida. All the state names confuse me. Even the numbered streets don't make sense. How can we go this far just to get from Twelfth Street to Eleventh Street? It seems to me one ought to be just a block beyond the other. Here's Eleventh Street now. Shall I turn?"

"Not yet," Liz objected. "This is the wrong Eleventh Street."

"Are there two of them?" Judy asked in amazement.

Liz giggled nervously. "It is confusing, isn't it? But we'll get home all right if you follow my directions, and you'll see a new part of Washington. That beautiful building with arches over the street is the Department of Agriculture."

"Do we go under the arches?"

"No, we turn here. This is Twelfth Street. You drive over the tracks."

"Is that so I can see the beautiful scenery to my left?" Judy asked suspiciously. "It looks like a freight yard."

"Drive right past it."

"With pleasure." Judy consulted the sky. Clouds were rolling up from the west. Or was it the east? She had lost all sense of direction. "Is that Maine Avenue up ahead where all the construction is going on?" she asked.

"Oh dear!" Liz exclaimed. "We'll have to detour down Avenue E. I'd forgotten Avenue F was all torn up like this. There's a new freeway being built along here. Do you mind?"

"I don't mind how many freeways they build," Judy replied impatiently. "I just want to get home before we're caught in a downpour. I have a feeling you've misdirected me on purpose. Tell me the truth, Liz. Is this really the way back to the motel?"

CHAPTER XIV

Empty Houses

"It's one way." Liz paused a long moment before she added, "I hope you'll remember it, Judy. You may be coming this way again."

"I doubt it. I avoid roads like this whenever I can. If it rains, all this mud from the construction will make it slippery, but what can I do?" asked Judy. "I'm so confused now that you'll have to direct me."

"Then turn right and drive down the next block in this same direction." Liz took a deep breath and rushed on. "You asked me to tell the truth, Judy, and I will. I suspected there might be a raid at the motel when I saw that glass paperweight. I was asked to find out if Peter was an FBI agent. Naturally, when I saw him about to guide the tour with his identification around his neck, I knew he was. And then, when he left so suddenly, I was pretty sure he'd been ordered to round up the gang. Charlie is one of them. Do you know where I got that information?"

Judy shook her head, too bewildered to reply.

"From you. Where else? Everything I know about the gang I learned from you. Charlie was afraid to tell me anything. He did give me an address, though. The house is along here somewhere. I'll tell you when we come to it. And please, please remember the house number. It's terribly important."

"I'll remember it," Judy promised, wondering what was coming next. Probably a shower. Thunder rumbled in the distance. The sky darkened, and the air grew heavy. There was something more in the air— something Judy was supposed to understand, but couldn't. Liz had a way of putting things so that you never quite knew what she really meant.

"Here it is, Judy," Liz said. "Stop here. I should only be a minute," she added. "If I'm too long, you'll know Charlie's there and I may be—I mean I may not be riding back with you."

"But Liz, you can't do this to me," Judy protested. "You were going to direct me. You know I can't find my way home from here."

"I told you," Liz insisted. "You drive along Maine to M, along M to Eleventh, to Maryland and along

Maryland to New York, and there you are at the motel."

"Maine, M, Eleventh, Maryland," Judy repeated. "I hope I can find it. How long shall I wait for you?"

"Don't wait long. This has been a good joke on me, really. I was supposed to be spying on you. Maybe you didn't know that, but I was. And now I'm actually begging you to spy on me."

"I don't know what you mean, Liz. I don't understand—"

"You will. Don't wait more than ten minutes. And Judy, this is important. Tell Peter everything I told you. And I mean *everything*. Is that clear?"

"About as clear as the weather," observed Judy, "but I'll certainly tell him."

"Thanks!" And Liz hurried off.

Judy saw her run up a long flight of steps, pause for a moment at a door with a number over it and then enter a building. It was a tall, unattractive red brick building that looked like a tenement. Glancing up, Judy noticed that there were no curtains at any of the windows. It looked deserted.

"It can't be," she whispered. "Why would Liz meet someone in an empty building?"

She memorized the number as she waited. Three minutes passed. Then the rain came, pelting against the windshield. Four minutes passed. Then five minutes. Judy waited, glancing from the clock on the dashboard panel to the silent house being lashed by the sudden rain.

Lightning flashed, brilliantly sharp, and all at once Judy noticed something else. The house where Liz had been admitted seemed empty, but the house next to it was just as deserted. The windows were black like watching eyes. Judy shivered. She tried to tell herself that she must be imagining the empty look to the row of houses. Liz couldn't visit someone who wasn't there.

But the door had been opened. Judy had distinctly seen it swing inward as someone let Liz in. Maybe it was the dark sky and the heavy air that made her feel something was wrong. And yet she knew in her heart that something had been wrong from the moment she met Liz. An undercurrent of fear had been expressed in her flippant words.

"I'll have to find out what's keeping her," Judy told herself at last.

Bending her head against the rain, she ran across the slippery walk and up those long, dismal steps. She would never forget this house, neither its appearance nor its number. She rang the bell, but it made no sound inside the empty rooms.

"The bell must be broken, or else the electricity is turned off," she decided, knocking with her fist against the door. It had no knocker. She tapped on the glass after peering through it to see nothing but a deserted hallway with another long flight of steps at the end.

There were no lights in the building. Judy banged on the door again and then turned the rusty doorknob. "Locked," she whispered in disappointment. "I was afraid it would be."

And yet someone had let Liz in. Charlie? Probably. No doubt they had met there by prearrangement, and the Beetle had served as a convenient taxi. Angry now, Judy banged harder, not expecting an answer, not getting one.

Slowly she walked down the steep steps. The house was empty. Every house on the whole street was empty, she saw, as she drove on past them. Some had already been leveled by steam shovels still standing there like dragons in the rain.

"Which way?" Judy asked herself.

This was F Street, a broken sign told her. Suddenly she remembered a map in the glove compartment. Consulting it, she finally found F Street marked: *Inner Loop Freeway Under Construction.* Those houses were condemned and were soon to be demolished. That was obvious. It was also obvious that Liz knew it and that she had taken Judy there on purpose. Had she wanted to lose her?

No, that couldn't be her reason. Her directions back to the motel seemed to be right. But something was wrong, terribly wrong, and Liz wanted her to know it. Judy could see on the map how far out of the way she had been taken. And that house number! Why had Liz insisted that Judy remember the number of a vacant house?

"I'll find Peter and bring him back here," Judy decided. "Then we'll see what's going on in those empty houses."

She found Maine Avenue and followed it past fish wharves and docks jutting out into gray water that seemed to be one with the gray, rainy sky. Other cars swished past, sure of where they were going. Judy drove on and would have missed M Street except that she saw other cars were turning.

Following them, Judy was relieved to see green trees ahead. Soon she was driving past Lincoln Square with its beautiful statue of Emancipation. A few blocks farther on she found Maryland Avenue slanting into Eleventh Street and turned east. She was driving along, confident that she would soon be at the motel when she glanced at the street sign and saw: *Bladensburg Road.*

"What happened?" she asked herself.

Hailing a passing car, she asked directions to Maryland Avenue.

"You're on it," the driver called back, laughing.

Judy didn't know what to make of it. "I need a guide," she thought, "but not Liz Holbrook." It was strange, but she still thought of the girl as a friend. And yet Liz had admitted that she was supposed to be spying on Judy! Why? Had her husband suspected who Peter was and sent Liz to find out? Or had she been spying for Mr. Rocklin? And why on earth would she turn the tables so suddenly and ask Judy to spy on her?

Puzzled by more than the strange street name, Judy pulled over to the curb and unfolded the map. Now she was sure of one thing, at least. Maryland Avenue and Bladensburg Road were one and the same. The highway, whatever its name, did cross New York Avenue. Judy felt like Columbus discovering America when she finally found the motel.

"At last!" she breathed, parking the Beetle before their door and pausing with mixed feelings of anticipation and dread. Had her wish come true? Would Blackberry be there waiting for her? Or would the room be empty like those houses?

"Liz was wrong," Judy told herself with determination. "I'll never want to go that way again."

CHAPTER XV

An Unsuccessful Raid

JUDY was just about to unlock the door with the key she had been carrying around all day in her pocketbook when, to her complete surprise and utter amazement, Peter emerged from the door right next to hers. She stared at him for a moment, unable to speak.

"What's the matter, Angel?" he asked, his blue eyes twinkling at her. "Didn't you expect to see me visiting our neighbors?"

"I certainly didn't. What were you doing in there?" Judy asked in alarm. "It wasn't a raid, was it?"

"You would have thought so if you'd been here a little earlier," he replied. "We had the place sur-

rounded. From what I overheard last night—"
"But Peter, you were asleep," Judy protested. "I
was the one who was bothered by all that talking."
"It's all on tape, thanks to you," Peter told her.
"Maybe you didn't notice a workman repairing the
cement in that passageway shortly after you showed
me the exact spot where you overheard that threat.
It was a simple matter to loosen one of those cement blocks and hide a tape recorder behind it. When
we played back the tape this morning we decided to
make a few arrests. But you're right. It wasn't much
of a raid."

"I'm glad." Judy stopped herself. Maybe she
shouldn't be glad. An unsuccessful raid was nothing
to be glad about. "I mean," she explained, "I'm glad
you're here and that you didn't get hurt or—or anything."

"You can say that again!" Peter exclaimed ruefully.
"I didn't get anything. I had another agent and a detail of policemen with me. We hoped we'd be interrupting a meeting of the syndicate, but somebody
must have tipped them off that we were on our way.
The room was vacant, just as you see it. So was the
restaurant."

"Are you talking about the restaurant here in the
motel?" asked Judy. "I hope it isn't closed."

"No, it's doing business as usual. I noticed a menu
posted in the window. Their southern fried chicken

looked good. Are you hungry?" Peter questioned.

"I'm starved," confessed Judy. "Can't we have something to eat while we talk things over? There's something I have to tell you. It was my fault about the raid. I know it was. Oh, Peter! I'm so ashamed."

"Of what?" he asked. "I'm rather proud of you myself. I always have been. Your confession can wait, can't it? I'm hungry, too."

They stopped in their room only long enough to freshen up for dinner. Judy's wish hadn't come true. A sharp pang of disappointment swept over her when she saw the empty room.

"Blackberry isn't here. I didn't really think he would be," she added wistfully. "I should have wished something a little more likely to come true."

"I did my best on this one," Peter told her, "but I guess this just isn't my lucky day."

"Mine either. It's been a weird one all right, but not very lucky. If I hadn't met Liz Holbrook—"

"Liz Holbrook?" Peter interrupted curiously. "Who's she?"

"Wait! Just wait and I'll tell you. I spent the whole afternoon with her and took her to visit someone in a row of empty houses. She said her Charlie might be there. She's only seventeen years old, but she's married to Charlie Caro. He is the man we saw right here when we registered. You know, the man who gave me such a funny look when I said the word *eagle*.

Liz works on the switchboard, but today she's off."

"It must be everybody's day off," Peter commented. "The motel certainly quieted down fast. The Rocklins seem to have disappeared along with everybody else. I did have some questions to ask them. But continue. What was it that made your day so weird?"

"It was everything!" declared Judy. "By the time we visited those empty houses, I'd really had it. Liz took me to them. I mean I took her, but she was directing me. She followed me on the FBI tour and pretended her husband was a G-man, too. I told her a lot of things I wouldn't have mentioned otherwise. I'm sorry, Peter," Judy finished, truly penitent. "Will you forgive me?"

"I may." Peter patted her arm reassuringly. She had just changed into a summer dress that made her look bewitching. Her gray eyes had a way of changing color to match the colors she wore. Suddenly they filled with tears. Peter pretended not to notice. "I have to hear the whole story," he added more gently, "before I know what I have to forgive."

"The whole story?" Judy questioned, turning her face away and dabbing at her eyes. "I hope I can tell it. That's what Liz said. She wanted me to tell you everything she'd told me. But there was so much and it's so mixed up in my mind. I don't know where to begin."

"The beginning will do very nicely."

Judy laughed, and the tears vanished. Peter made it all sound so simple.

"Shall I begin when Liz first spoke to me?" she asked. "I think she'd been watching me long before that. She admitted she was a spy for someone, and she scared me pink telling me you were out on a raid. I had visions of you shooting it out with her Charlie and leaving him dead or else getting shot yourself. I even thought of that criminal syndicate you mentioned and wondered if they could be meeting in those empty houses. Something strange is going on there. Maybe, if you had raided them instead of this motel, you might have found something."

"It could be." Peter seemed to be keeping something back. Judy felt sure it was something he dreaded telling her. He said he'd keep the houses in mind. But afterwards she couldn't remember having told him where they were.

"Ready?" he asked as she gave her hair a final pat and turned toward the long mirror in their room to see if her dress hung just right. Peter smiled at this feminine gesture.

"You don't need to laugh at me," Judy flared. "I have to look right when I feel so guilty. Did I tell you Liz practically begged me to spy on her because— well, I guess she must be taking orders from Charlie, and he's taking them from his employer, who has been forced into crime. She said something about a cousin who had married into the family just the way she did. They're both related to the Rocklins. They may be in the syndicate themselves. But I guess that's too fantastic, isn't it?"

Judy had noticed a look of skepticism on Peter's face.

"Aren't you getting a little ahead of your story?" he asked. "What makes you think Charlie takes orders from his employer?"

"Liz told me after she grew confidential. She first spoke to me after she saw the glass paperweight with the fingerprints on it," Judy explained. "I was so surprised I guess I did say something about its coming from this motel. She heard me, and I had a feeling, just at first, that she might know something about it. Then she began to pretend—"

"That her husband was one of our agents?"

Peter asked the question in a low voice, reminding Judy to keep her own voice down as they entered the motel lobby. They had to pass through it on their way to the dining room unless they used the passageway. Peter avoided this route although it was a little longer walk around to the front door. The court beyond the dining room was deserted because of the rain, and all the outdoor tables were stripped of their plaid tablecloths.

"It looks different, doesn't it?" observed Judy.

"Not quite so gay as it did when we first came in. I thought then that it was a little too modern. Now it just looks bare and empty. I'm glad there are a few people in the main dining room."

"Let's sit here where we can look them over," Peter suggested, choosing a center table.

Judy gave him a puzzled look. She would have preferred one of the booths against the wall or a table by the window. Nobody else was sitting near them. Perhaps that was why Peter chose this particular table. He wanted to hear the rest of Judy's story.

Their orders were taken and their plates on the table before she had finished telling him the events of the mystifying day that was ending.

"I remembered my wish after you left," Judy confided. "You know, the one I said I'd forgotten. It was a wish for Senator Hockett's safety. I told you I thought that Statuary Hall must be haunted, didn't I? Well, afterwards, I put two and two together and figured out why."

Peter agreed with Judy that the whisper must have come from across the floor where the three men were plotting against the senator.

"You should have reported it to me at once—"

"But Peter," Judy protested, "it didn't seem real at first. It seemed as if the statues were whispering. I couldn't report that. And afterwards, when I realized it might be those men talking, I couldn't find you. Liz said you were probably out on a raid."

"She was right. I hope she was only guessing. The Bureau doesn't like to have its plans leak out. Now, of course, it's public knowledge. To tell you the truth, we expected trouble, but there was nothing at all suspicious. Nothing," he ended, "except one small clue." He held it up. Judy gasped in astonishment.

"Blackberry's collar!" she exclaimed. "Where did you find it?"

CHAPTER XVI

A Revelation

"Was it in that motel room?" Judy persisted when Peter did not answer immediately.

He shook his head. "No, we found it in a restaurant. It was hidden in the back of the cash drawer. The owner probably intended to pawn the gold medal. We're holding him for questioning, but he will probably be released soon," Peter predicted. "It's just as he says. You can't make a federal case out of a missing cat."

"But now Blackberry has no identification!" Judy thought of Rosita's promise. "The manager's daughter said Blackberry was taken to a restaurant. She couldn't remember the name—"

"Krut's Rotisserie is quite a mouthful," agreed Peter. "That tape gave us a lot of clues and a long list of names that will help us round up these gangsters. We weren't looking for a cat's collar. A raid is serious business. Your friend Liz must have realized that."

"She did. I was so worried about you, Peter, and she seemed just as worried about her husband. I thought she might know something, working on the switchboard and all, so I asked her about Blackberry. She didn't tell me anything but, somehow, she acted guilty and right afterwards she made a telephone call."

"You don't know whom she called, do you?"

"No, but it could have been the Rocklins." It didn't seem likely, though, when Judy thought about it. "Maybe she tipped off the people in the restaurant," she added. "Oh dear! I guess I did talk too much."

"It could be," Peter agreed with a whimsical smile.

"How can you smile about it?" cried Judy. "It's true! Maybe I did help you plan where to put the tape recorder, but then I had to go and spoil everything by exclaiming over that paperweight. I suspect Liz knew whose fingerprints were on it. Her Charlie must be up to his ears in crime, and I had to blab everything to Liz and keep you from arresting him. I'm not at all like the good wife described in the folder Mr. Gunn gave me. She wasn't curious about her husband's work. She didn't ask questions and she didn't make a hobby of solving mysteries—"

"And I didn't marry her," Peter interrupted. "Maybe you aren't the Bureau's idea of what a good wife should be, but you're mine."

"Am I really?"

Peter nodded. "I wouldn't change a hair in your gorgeous head."

"You'd shut my gorgeous mouth if you could. It hurts worse when you're so sweet about it," declared Judy. "I could bite off my tongue for some of the things I said."

"Please don't, not until you've finished your dinner, anyway," implored Peter. "You said you were hungry, but you're not eating. Isn't the chicken good?"

"It's delicious," declared Judy.

They ate for a while in silence. The restaurant was less crowded than usual. Judy glanced at the wall clock, decorated with eagles, and saw that it was a little late for dinner. Maybe that was why everything seemed to be waiting, almost as if some blow were about to fall.

"Were there many people in the restaurant you raided?" asked Judy, forgetting that a good FBI wife isn't curious.

"Not many."

Suddenly Peter excused himself to make a telephone call. Judy was used to this as he had to call in regularly when he was out on an assignment.

"He's still on this one," she thought, vaguely uneasy. Now she knew why he had taken that particular table. He had been watching the people entering and leaving the dining room.

Judy felt a little conspicuous sitting alone waiting for him. Several people turned to look at her. Were they admiring her dress, or was her zipper unfastened at the back? There was no one in the restaurant that she knew or had ever seen before except—

Judy blinked and looked again. There, seated at one of the tables, quietly eating her dinner, was Liz with her Charlie. It was the same young man Judy had seen earlier.

"They didn't stay long in the empty house," Judy thought.

Liz hadn't looked at her. Judy lowered her own eyes, not wanting to stare. It was good to know that Liz was all right, and yet a nagging doubt persisted.

"Sorry, sweetheart," Peter said, returning from the telephone booth. "It's official business. I'll have to leave you to spend the evening alone. You can look at television—"

"No, thanks. To tell you the truth, I'm tired," Judy admitted. "I'll probably take a nap and be all rested and wide awake when you come in too tired to talk."

"Do that," Peter advised her. "I'll listen. By the way, I reported that threat to Senator Hockett."

"Good!" applauded Judy. She thought a minute. "Isn't there something else you ought to report? I mean about those empty houses. Liz wanted me to come back with you, but now I guess we can forget it. There she is, with her Charlie. They're sitting over there by the window."

"I noticed them."

"You did? Is that why you made the telephone call?"

"Curious," he scolded. "You know I have to call in my reports. I can't wait for dessert. Order some for yourself, and keep an eye on your friend. 'Bye for now. I'll see you around midnight."

" 'Bye, Peter. Take care."

He was gone before Judy had a chance to ask him what he meant. Should she pretend not to know Liz or go over and greet her? She didn't look like a girl in need of help. Charlie's back was toward Judy, but Liz was looking over the top of Judy's head as if she were a stranger.

"She doesn't want me to recognize her—not while she's with Charlie," Judy decided.

Still wondering what was expected of her, she finished her dessert and picked up the money Peter had left her to pay the check. She was at the cashier's booth counting her change when she heard a hiss in her ear: "Where's Peter?"

"He had to leave. He'll be back soon," Judy whispered in a voice so low she wasn't sure even Liz could hear her.

There was no answer. Liz was tracing out the house

number in the air when Charlie turned and asked suspiciously, "What are you up to?"

"It's a fly. It keeps bothering me. I wish you'd *hurry* . . ."

Liz and Charlie left the restaurant, still talking, apparently of something else. But that one word was meant for her. Judy knew it. Liz had given her just one imploring glance. It was only on the surface that everything appeared to be all right. The undercurrent of fear had grown stronger.

"I hope Peter does hurry," she thought. "Something is wrong, and he ought to know about it. I'll tell him the minute he comes in."

Judy wandered around the motel lobby hoping she would see Rosita. But she saw no one except strangers going in and out.

Tomorrow, she hoped, Liz would be back at the switchboard. Maybe they could become real friends. Judy needed a few friends in Washington with Peter gone all day. Seeing the sights with Liz would be fun. Or would it? Judy had not cared very much for the sights they had seen on the way to those empty houses.

"Was Liz trying to lead me into a trap?" she wondered.

It seemed unlikely. The day had been long—too long, and Judy was suddenly tired. She went to the room that seemed so empty without Blackberry and turned on the television. She knew Irene Meredith and some of the others who appeared on her Saturday night program. But this was only Tuesday, and none of the Tuesday night shows interested her.

At home, when she watched television Blackberry was usually purring in her lap. He didn't watch unless there was some quick movement on the screen. Then he would jump down and peer behind the set as if he expected to catch whatever it was that moved. Thinking of his peculiar cat ways made Judy miss him more than ever. She hadn't expected a miracle just because she had wished for it. But, somehow, she hadn't expected this emptiness and this silence. Suddenly, a few minutes later, the silence was shattered by a thunderous knock on the door.

"Who is it?" cried Judy. She had been resting on the bed, and the knock had startled her. It couldn't be Peter. He would tap gently or use his key.

"It is I, Anthony Rocklin," a man's voice answered.

Judy heard herself gasp in sudden dread. What did he want? Could he be returning Blackberry? Then Judy heard a babble of excited voices outside her door. The manager's voice was raised above the others.

"Open up!" he called. "I must see you."

Hardly knowing what to expect, Judy's hand moved toward the doorknob.

"I must see you, too, Mr. Rocklin," she exclaimed, opening the door. "What's all the commotion? We received your note last night. You said the cat was returned, but all my husband found was his collar. Will you please tell me where—"

She was not allowed to finish. It was a simple question she had started to ask. Mr. Rocklin might know the answer. Judy was not prepared for the outburst that followed. Mrs. Rocklin joined in. Judy could see that she had been weeping. Her words were incoherent. The other relatives stood around in a hostile semicircle. It was Mr. Rocklin who shouted, " 'Where is my cat?' she asks! She is looking for a cat! What do you think—I should help you find your cat when my daughter is missing?"

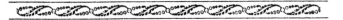

CHAPTER XVII

The Accusers Accused

"Your daughter? You mean Rosita?" gasped Judy. "Why, I saw her only this morning. She was touring the Capitol Building with her class—"

"That's right!" sobbed Mrs. Rocklin. "The teacher didn't watch her. Did you take my Rosita? Where did you take her? Where?"

Judy stood there bewildered. Blinking in the sudden light that she turned on in order to see her accusers, she felt trapped and helpless. She thought that she must have fallen asleep waiting for Peter. To be awakened so suddenly and faced with a barrage of accusations was just too much. Mrs. Rocklin kept on sobbing.

"Wait, Mamma! Give her time to answer," Mr. Rocklin said more reasonably.

Judy saw some hope of explaining things to Mr. Rocklin as soon as she had figured them out for herself.

It had happened, the thing Liz had feared. Judy had to think back. She had to remember every detail of that strange morning in the Capitol. She had seen Rosita join her classmates. She had heard her call out a cheerful "See you?" after promising to find out the name of the restaurant where Blackberry had been taken. Maybe she had gone there and somehow, during the raid, become lost. Perhaps she had followed the cat and they would be found together.

"Did she go to the restaurant where my cat was?" Judy asked hopefully.

"No! No! We looked there. We looked everywhere. She never came home from school. The teacher says *you* stopped her."

"Of course, Mrs. Rocklin, but I only stopped her for a minute—"

"A minute! An hour! What is the difference?"

"The restaurant has been closed up," Mr. Rocklin snapped. "Raided, they told me. I don't suppose you knew anything about that?"

"Why, no, I—I didn't—"

"Innocent, aren't you?" sneered one of the watchers. Judy didn't know whether or not he was a member of Rosita's family, but it was a voice Judy had heard before.

"Yes, I am innocent," she retorted, "and I think you know it. I heard you talking with someone yesterday. I was walking along that passageway back of the laundry when I heard you say—"

"You heard nothing," the man interrupted. "I don't know what you're talking about."

"No?" Judy realized she must be cautious. If this man did turn out to be the criminal she had heard directing someone to make it look like an accident, she could be inviting trouble.

"Cousin Vin, have you met this girl?" asked the first relative who had spoken.

"Never," he replied, "but the cat was in her room, quite obviously planted."

Judy did not either confirm or deny this. She could see it was hopeless to try the strategy she and Peter had planned. She couldn't pretend to be anything but what she was—a bewildered girl accused without reason. Or was there a reason? Six words flashed back from that conversation she had overheard in Statuary Hall: "*I'll be back with the kid.*"

Had the man returned? Judy had caught only a glimpse of him across the hall, but he could be the same man who was accusing her now. Rosita would have gone with a cousin willingly. But where would he have taken her? And what about Charlie and the two men waiting with him?

"Those empty houses!" Judy exclaimed.

Suddenly she had the answer. The FBI tour with Liz spying on her and then the tables turning, Liz's confession, her sudden haste. It all made sense now. Liz was afraid for Rosita!

"Empty houses, you say? Where?" Mr. Rocklin's voice rose shrilly. "Tell them I'll pay—"

"How can I tell them when I don't know who they are?" Judy broke in. "You were mistaken when you wrote that note. Nobody sent us to frighten you with our cat, but we can help you if you'll let us."

"I said I'd pay—"

"We don't want your money. Please believe me," implored Judy. "This is real help I'm offering. You don't have to pay for it. The law will protect you."

"I dare not go to the law." Mr. Rocklin was firm about this. "A restaurant was burned to the ground. A man was pushed from a window. You don't know these people, what they do—"

"Wait, Mr. Rocklin," Judy stopped him. "I do know. Let me tell you what I think really happened. What Rosita's teacher told you is true. I am the girl who spoke to her this morning when she was touring the Capitol Building with her class. But it was someone else who took her. I heard a man say he would be 'back with the kid.' "

"You think this man has her?"

"Not now." Judy looked directly at the relative she suspected. "He probably left her with one of the other men. Charlie, perhaps. You do have a nephew named Charlie, don't you, Mr. Rocklin?"

"He's my wife's brother's boy. He lives here with us when he's in the city. He's married—"

"I know," Judy interrupted quietly. "To a girl named Liz. I met her this afternoon and told her just what I'm telling you. Her Charlie, as she calls him, and two other men were waiting upstairs in the Capitol Building just about the time Rosita must have disappeared."

"Walter Krut led him into this," Mr. Rocklin said bitterly. "No wonder Krut's place was raided. Vincent Norton here works for him, Mamma. Naturally Charlie trusts his cousin's employer."

"I see." Judy spoke to Mr. Rocklin directly as she described the men she had seen waiting under the chariot clock.

"They were all dark-haired except the one who said he'd 'be back with the kid.' He was big and blond—the outdoor type," she finished.

"Don't know him," Mr. Rocklin muttered although Judy's description did fit the blond relative to whom he had referred as Vincent Norton. "Vin married a distant cousin of ours. They're all good people," Mr. Rocklin declared. "They wouldn't hurt my little Rosita. Charlie treats her like a sister. Are you telling me the truth? Was Charlie with them?"

"Yes, I'm sure he was." Judy could see that Charlie was a favorite with Mr. Rocklin. All the time she was talking, Mrs. Rocklin kept her beady eyes upon her. All the others stared at her, too—a barrage of accusation.

"Trying to shift the blame," one said and the others

agreed with this sentiment. There were two women in the group who hadn't spoken, but their silence spoke for them. Judy could feel their distrust of her, an outsider, a stranger. Vincent Norton was the one they trusted.

"Aren't you going to do anything about this, Mr. Rocklin?" Judy asked in amazement. "Rosita may be in danger. I think they've taken her to one of a row of empty houses that are about to be demolished—"

"An accident!" screamed Mrs. Rocklin. "They'll make it look like an accident! Go, Papa! Quick, before the house falls on her."

"I'll show you the way," Judy offered. "You can follow me in your car."

"No, no, you can't trust her." Vincent Norton, the man she had accused, whispered something to Mr. Rocklin. He glanced fearfully past Judy toward the room behind her. "Was your husband with you?" he demanded.

"If you mean when I toured the Capitol this morning, the answer is no. I was alone when I saw those men and heard them plotting. I thought their plot was against a senator. They whispered a watchword, but if Rosita—"

"Don't say it!" Mr. Rocklin groaned. "I will pay, Mamma. It was foolish of me to hold out so long."

"It is too late. I feel it here." Mrs. Rocklin touched her heart. "You must pay, but already it is too late."

"It can't be!" cried Judy. "Ask *him*. He knows."

She pointed an accusing finger at Vincent Norton. "You can't trust him," she insisted. "Just because he married into your family—"

"He is one of us now," one of the women spoke quietly to defend him.

"I've told everything I know," Judy said fervently. "Liz said to hurry—"

"Ah! So she did follow you?" Mr. Rocklin exclaimed.

"Did you ask her to, Mr. Rocklin? I'm glad of that," declared Judy. "Then you know—"

"I know you've been spying on us. We didn't invite government snoopers to interfere—"

"It's about time somebody interfered," Judy interrupted angrily. "If my husband doesn't come home soon, I think you ought to notify the police—"

"No!" She got no farther. The interruption came from all the throats. The circle of watching eyes accused Judy in spite of the evidence.

"If you won't go back there, I will," Judy decided. She wrote the house number on a slip of paper and handed it to Mr. Rocklin. "This is where I'm going. I want my husband to know it. Tell him the house looks empty so he will know what to expect."

Hardly knowing what to expect herself, Judy slid behind the wheel of her car and drove off into the night.

CHAPTER XVIII

Discovered!

On her way to the empty houses Judy had time to realize to the full the chance she was taking. Unable to do anything herself without arousing Charlie's suspicions, Liz was depending on her. But she was depending on Peter, too!

Doubts began to assail Judy. She was driving back the way she had come, a little more sure of the direction but less sure than ever that she had made the right decision. If she had waited another five minutes, perhaps, Peter might have returned. Then, again, he might not. He could have been waiting outside with another agent to pick up Charlie Caro when he left the motel restaurant. Had he picked up Liz, too?

"I shouldn't have acted so impulsively," Judy told

herself. "And yet, how could I have waited?" Mrs. Rocklin might be right and in another five minutes it would be too late. Judy felt sure now that Rosita was in real danger.

"Liz thinks I'm trying to get ahead of Peter, to compete with him," she remembered.

It was a disquieting thought. As she approached the row of dark, deserted houses Judy began to wish she had not come alone. There wasn't a sign of life anywhere. She parked the Beetle at the curb. No other cars were parked on the empty street. There were no lights in any of the houses.

Judy had brought her flashlight. Shining it on the house number Liz had been so afraid she would forget, she started up the long steps to the door. Once there, she paused, wondering if she should knock and half dreading the sound of her own rapping and the echoes that might be called forth from the empty house. If Rosita had been imprisoned in one of the rooms, there would be no one to open the door. She tried it and was not surprised to find it locked.

"I'll try the windows," she decided.

One of them had been broken. Boards had been nailed across it but they came away easily when Judy inserted another board between the cracks and pried with all her strength. She heard the tearing sound of the nails as they came loose and knew she had been successful. The boards were a help, too, when she climbed inside. The first sound she heard was that of breaking glass as she let herself down inside one of the basement rooms.

"Rosita!" she called softly, not expecting an answer. The room had a closed-in, musty odor. The beam from Judy's flashlight showed her nothing but the littered floor, bare of furniture, and a wooden door with cracked panels leading to the next room.

"Probably it's bare like this one," Judy thought as she entered. Was that a refrigerator blocking her way? She flashed her light on it and recognized a slot machine. Beyond it was another and then another. In all, there were six machines stored in the basement room. Judy knew such machines were used for gambling and that they were illegal in all but a few states. Certainly such machines were against the law in the nation's capital.

"Could these be the machines Peter expected to find when he raided that restaurant?" Judy asked herself. "Did Liz know they would be here?"

If gambling machines were all that had been hidden in the empty house she could have waited until morning. She didn't really care if those machines were demolished when the wreckers came. Peter would know why they were there. Judy found herself listening for his footsteps.

In another room she found an old desk and a group of chairs. It looked almost as if this were a conference room. A wastebasket filled with papers might yield some interesting clues.

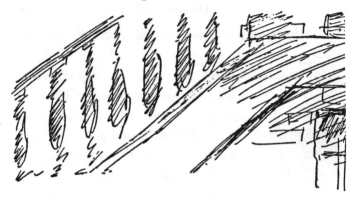

"What on earth is this?" she whispered to herself, unfolding one of the crumpled papers. Her flashlight showed her that it was a crude map or plan of the ground floor of a motel or night club. She couldn't be sure which. Squares and circles with criss-crosses over them represented tables. These were easy to identify. The other squares and oblongs were more difficult.

"I'll keep this map and study it," Judy decided. "It may show me where those gambling machines came from."

Some of the squares could be gambling machines. They were marked with names—Krut, Norton, Ceron . . .

"That's interesting," Judy thought, folding the crumpled paper and tucking it away in her purse.

If Peter came he would probably want to take the whole wastebasket to the Document Section where its contents could be examined scientifically. Judy was convinced, by now, that this room had been the meeting place for the criminal syndicate after they had been warned of the raid. She felt elated at her discovery. But what other secret was the empty house hiding?

Her flashlight making ghostly circles on floor, walls, and ceiling, Judy searched each one of the basement rooms. She opened closets and built-in

cupboards. Each time she opened a door her heart beat fast for fear of what she might discover.

Turning from the cavernous silence of the basement,

she crept up the stairs to the main floor. Here she had to be a little more cautious with her flashlight. Suppose someone should see the beam and, knowing the house was supposed to be empty, start to investigate? Judy would have a difficult time explaining her presence there.

"Except to Peter. I could explain it to him fast enough," she thought, wishing he would come.

Searching through these empty rooms was beginning to give her the same shivery feeling she had experienced among the statues. No sound came from any of the rooms except the creaking of rusty hinges as she opened door after door, finding nothing but bare rooms and empty closets and occasionally a broken piece of abandoned furniture.

She unlocked the front door, just in case Peter did come, and felt better until she realized that she had also unlocked it for anyone who might wish to slip inside.

"Who would?" she asked herself.

It was a question she didn't dare answer. She had asked Mr. Rocklin to follow her, but he was afraid. What was it, then, that gave her courage? She stood quite still for a moment feeling, as she often felt, that she was never quite alone. It was the knowledge that she was doing right that gave her courage. She had been too impulsive, perhaps, but her motives were good. Breathing a silent prayer for Rosita, she continued her search.

Upstairs a white bathtub sitting in the hall startled her. The plumbing had been disconnected. Broken windows let in night-flying insects that flitted about her flashlight and brushed against her face. "Nothing," she kept repeating to herself as she opened the doors. Once this building must have housed five or six families. It seemed strange that anybody could have lived in these rooms and made them cheerful. They were now utterly devoid of light and cheer.

"Rosita can't be in this awful building. I'm just scaring myself wandering around," Judy thought as she climbed the last flight of rickety steps and reached the top floor. Far below she could hear the sound of a truck rumbling along the street. Looking out, she saw nothing but the Beetle waiting at the curb. Torn up as it was, there probably was little traffic on this street even in the daytime.

"I'll go back to the motel as soon as I've looked in these rooms," Judy decided, opening the first door.

No sooner had she made this resolution than she heard, or fancied she heard, the sound of something banging downstairs. Quick as a flash she was inside the room with the door closed. Leaning against the panel, she stood for a moment listening.

"Nothing," she scolded herself. "You're hearing things, Judy girl. You'd better get out of here before you develop a case of nerves."

There were only two more rooms to be explored. Judy dreaded going into them. Her hope that she might learn something about Rosita's disappearance became a fear that she might not. For a full minute this fear kept her from turning the knob of the last door.

As she stood there in the dark with only the small circle from her flashlight playing on the door, a stealthy footstep sounded from somewhere in the empty house.

"Peter? Is that you?" Judy called uncertainly.

There was no answer.

"Mr. Rocklin?"

This time the silence welled up around Judy, filling her with fear. Why didn't the man answer? She knew it must be a man because of the heavy footstep. But it was no friend. She felt sure of that. It wasn't even a friendly stranger. Judy snapped off her flashlight, backed against the wall and stood there petrified.

The man had an electric torch of some kind. Judy could see its light moving ahead of him as he mounted the stairs. He was walking stealthily, but occasionally a board would creak beneath his weight.

"He *mustn't* see me," Judy thought.

A flashlight beam played across the floor, missing her by inches. Edging along the wall, Judy groped for the doorknob. Whoever he was, he mustn't stop her from discovering what was in that room. Somehow, Judy felt that this was his purpose.

She knew it, minutes later, when his flashlight found her and his voice barked from out of the shadows, "Don't open that door!"

CHAPTER XIX

Locked In

THE order had an instant effect on Judy. Her natural curiosity overcame her fear. It was with a strange calmness that she whirled around and snapped her flashlight on the intruder's startled face.

"Vincent Norton!" she exclaimed. "I thought it would be you."

Judy had recognized his voice when he ordered her not to open the door. He must have come in through the front door she had left open for Peter. Or perhaps he had a key and could have come in anyway. Now he stood between her and the stairs, blocking her way.

"What are you doing here?" he demanded.

"You know what I'm doing," Judy retorted. "I'm

139

looking for Rosita just as I said I would. I asked Mr. Rocklin to follow me here, but I'm not sure you didn't prevent him. That *was* your voice I heard in the passageway back at the motel. Now I know it. I suspect you were talking to Charlie Caro. He was afraid to disobey you, wasn't he? Well, I'm not."

"You seem to know a lot about my affairs," Vincent Norton said sneeringly.

"On the contrary," Judy flared back, "I know very little, but I intend to find out. Why did you follow me here?"

"For the same reason I had Liz Holbrook follow you after she telephoned the restaurant," he replied harshly. "She found out you're one of the government's snoopers."

"I'm not—"

"Your husband is. It's all the same," declared Vincent Norton, his voice sounding loud and threatening in the empty house. "You report all your findings to him, don't you? Well, there's one find you won't report. It's that map you took from the wastebasket."

"Map?" Judy's bewilderment was genuine. She had momentarily forgotten the piece of crumpled paper she had put in her pocketbook.

"Don't pretend you didn't take it. Who else would?" Norton said sharply.

"Who else is here?" Judy retorted.

"Did you find anyone?"

"Not yet, but perhaps I will. If you will stand aside, please, I have one more door to open."

"You'll not open it!"

Norton's face became contorted with rage. He took a step toward Judy, but she was too quick for him. Opening the door, she slammed it shut and braced her body against it while she turned the night catch. In the excitement she had dropped her flashlight. She heard a chuckle of satisfaction as Norton picked it up.

"You'll find it dark in there, Mrs. Dobbs. But you won't have long to wait. The wreckers will be here early in the morning. You were just a little too curious," he added as he slid the bolt in place, locking the door from the outside as well. Still chuckling to himself, he turned and walked noisily downstairs.

Judy stood for a moment blinking her eyes and trying to see what sort of a room it was. It must be large and windowless. With both arms outstretched, she could find no walls. Not the faintest glow of light relieved the inky blackness.

"I'm not frightened," she thought, marveling that the fear had left her.

She knew that she was locked in. But, somehow, she had faith that someone would come. She had done what she thought was right, and it gave her confidence. The wreckers would not come to demolish the house until it was daylight. In the meantime, she could do some exploring in the dark.

"I'll think of it as an adventure," she resolved, continuing her search. She found one wall. It was papered, she discovered, and some of the wallpaper had come loose and was hanging in strips.

"A lovely room, I'm sure," she consoled herself. "Maybe it's just as well I can't see it."

This room had the same musty odor as all the others. Judy longed to open a window, if she could find one, and let in at least a glimmer of light and a little air from outside. She could touch the ceiling now. This part of the room seemed to be low, sloping toward the eaves.

"Another haunted attic!" she thought with a shiver. Suddenly from somewhere in the warm and stuffy room came a low moan. The sound came again. It would not have frightened Judy if she had been anywhere else. It was a very low moan, hardly more than a sigh. The wind, perhaps, though not a breath of air was stirring inside.

There must be a window in the room if only Judy could find it. Halfway around, she came to a jog in the wall. Yes, it was a low dormer window with the shade drawn. It ripped when she tried to raise it.

"Who cares?" she exclaimed aloud, tearing it off and discarding it. The floor was so littered that one more scrap wouldn't matter. The house was to be demolished, anyway. "With me in it," Judy thought in panic, "unless someone comes."

With the shade gone and the window raised, Judy could see the sky outside. Nothing else. But that glimpse of the sky with two faint stars twinkling through the clouds gave her hope. It was dark out there. But it was a clean, refreshing dark. Not the closed-in stuffiness of this room that had become her prison.

"There's no wind," she whispered, mystified. What had caused that faint moan as of a child sighing and turning over in its sleep?

The window let in only a little light. Nothing in the room appeared to have form or shape. After taking a deep breath of the fresh air that came in through the open window, Judy continued feeling her way, hoping against hope that there would be another door that was not locked or another stairway.

Once more she stopped to listen. Absolute stillness. Judy could hear nothing but the sound of her own breathing. Or was that her own? There was not the slightest indication of movement in the inky blackness that surrounded her. The window was a pale square in the dark, showing her nothing. And yet she felt, suddenly, that there must be someone else not far away.

"Rosita! Are you in here?"

Calling softly, Judy began to move cautiously toward the sound of breathing. Another step, and she stumbled against something that felt like cloth. She bent to touch it and drew back in alarm. What she had touched was human hair!

"Who is it?" she gasped. "Rosita, if that's you, speak to me."

The figure at her feet remained motionless and just as quiet as before. There was still the faint sound of regular breathing.

"Rosita," Judy whispered, kneeling beside her, and then softly to herself, "She's sound asleep!"

How could it be? Judy's trembling fingers found Rosita's face. They touched her warm cheek and moved over to her closed eyes. "It's Rosita all right," she said to herself. "I mustn't wake her. It would only frighten her. I'll just sit here beside her and wait."

A quilt, or something that felt like a quilt, had been thrown on the floor for a bed. Rosita had no cover. It was so warm she didn't need one. She seemed to be quite comfortable. Perhaps she had gone to sleep when it was still daylight. More likely she had been terrified and cried herself to sleep. She would be even more frightened if she awoke without someone to comfort her.

"I can do that much, anyway," thought Judy, seating herself beside her and gently stroking her hand. The younger girl sighed again in her sleep.

Minutes later, as Judy placed her hand on her damp forehead, Rosita murmured, "Is that you, Liz?" Then, rousing a little, she said dazedly, "I guess I went to

sleep listening to the story. Are we still in the empty
house?"

"Yes," Judy answered quietly, "we're still here.
When you wake up you can tell me about it."

"You're not Liz!" Rosita was suddenly filled with
panic. "Who are you? Why is it so dark? Liz and
Cousin Charlie were here when I went to sleep. Where
are they now?"

Judy wanted to know the answer to that question
herself.

"They sent me," she began. "You remember me,
Rosita? I spoke to you when you were on the tour—"

"You're the lady with the cat?"

"Yes, I met your cousin Liz, and she sent me here
to make sure you were all right. Go back to sleep,"
Judy advised, beginning to stroke Rosita's forehead.
She sang a little song remembered from childhood:

> "The friendly dark is all around
> When I'm in bed at night.
> It creeps on tiptoe through the room
> To take the place of light."

"I like that. The dark is friendly, isn't it?" Rosita
asked when the song was finished.

"It certainly is," Judy reassured her. The dark, she
thought to herself, was much more friendly than the
daylight when those pulleys and steam shovels would
come to demolish the houses.

CHAPTER XX

A New Danger

MINUTES stretched into what seemed like hours while Judy waited beside the sleeping Rosita. She didn't dare go to sleep herself for fear daylight would come without her being aware of it and, with daylight, those murderous machines. Would the men give the houses a final search before they were pulled down? Judy hoped so. She could bang on the door and shout to attract their attention. Banging and shouting now would be a waste of breath since there was no one around to hear.

With a sigh, Judy arose from her cramped position on the floor and walked over to the window. More stars had come out. The sky was clear. That was a hopeful sign. She could tell when morning came. "It mustn't come ahead of Peter," she thought. .

She found herself listening to every small sound, hoping it would be his footstep. Downstairs, somewhere, there was a creaking noise as of someone opening a door. Judy cupped her hands and shouted, "Peter, we're up here!"

Her shout had no effect except to stir up the echoes in the empty house and startle Rosita.

"What's the matter? Who's Peter?" she asked out of the dark corner where she had been sleeping.

"He's my husband."

"My goodness!" Rosita exclaimed, sitting up and reaching for Judy's comforting hand. "Are you married, too? I thought you were too young, but I guess you aren't. Liz is only seventeen, and she's married to Cousin Charlie."

"Did he bring you here?"

Rosita murmured something that sounded like a yes.

"That wasn't his voice I heard in Statuary Hall, but he's in on the plot against Senator Hockett, too," Judy thought. Would that, too, be made to look like an accident? Judy hoped she had told Peter about the whispered threat in time for him to stop whatever they were planning.

"Strange," she said aloud. "I still don't understand it."

"What don't you understand?" Rosita asked.

She was fully awake now. Possibly she was aware of something wrong. Judy knew she would have to keep talking.

"The whisper I heard," she replied. "Not here. In Statuary Hall. Rosita, did your class tour that room where all the statues are?"

Rosita assured Judy that they had. "I heard the whispers, too, but I've forgotten what makes them."

"The acoustics?"

"Yes, that was the word the guide used. We whispered back and forth and heard each other. The teacher said she'd explain it to the class later, but I didn't go back to school with them. Cousin Vin stopped me right after I saw you."

"Cousin Vin?"

"Yes, he's married to Cousin Anna, and she's nice. Mamma has a lot of relatives. I didn't think she'd care if I went with him. Cousin Vin said I didn't need to go back to school. It was the last day, you know. He took me back upstairs."

"To Statuary Hall?"

"Yes, that's where Cousin Charlie and two of his friends were waiting. I like Cousin Charlie. He asked me if I'd had a good time touring the Capitol. Then he said he'd show me some other sights. They're building a new freeway. All these houses are going to be torn down tomorrow. Did you know that?"

Judy gulped. "Er—yes, I know," she said.

"They said I could stand outside and watch the wreckers," Rosita chattered on.

"We'll both watch," Judy agreed. Her voice sounded cheerful, but she shuddered inwardly at the thought. They would be watching from *inside* the house if someone didn't come to rescue them soon.

"When will it be daylight?" Rosita asked after a short silence.

"Not for a long time . . . *I hope*," Judy added to herself. She thought she heard something downstairs. Now she was sure of it. She listened again. Clear and distinct from somewhere in the lower part of the house came the sound of something heavy being moved. "Those machines!" she exclaimed.

"Do you mean those machines you put money in? I saw them downstairs. Cousin Charlie says they're fixed so people always lose. They used to have one in the restaurant where Cousin Vin works, but Papa wouldn't let me play it."

"Is that the restaurant where they took my cat?"

"Yes, did you find him?"

"No, only his collar. Peter found that. You don't know where the cat is now, do you?"

"I asked Cousin Liz. She knows—"

"Are you sure, Rosita? It's strange she wouldn't tell me about Blackberry if she knows where he is."

"Ask her," Rosita suggested. "She'll be at the switchboard tomorrow."

There was another silence during which Judy could hear whoever was downstairs moving about. Voices floated up.

"That's Cousin Vin!" Rosita exclaimed.

He had just said, "We'll have to get rid of that," and now Judy could hear a new noise that put terror in her heart. It was a distinct crackling sound.

"I smell smoke. Is there a fire somewhere?" Rosita asked, jumping to her feet. She clung to Judy, terrified.

"Your cousin may be burning papers." Judy ran to the window and looked out. A red glow reflecting on the opposite wall from somewhere directly beneath her told her that there definitely was a fire.

"I think somebody *is* burning papers," she repeated to reassure Rosita.

"He may set the house afire. We'll have to get out of here. Do you have your car, Judy? May I call you Judy or would you rather I called you Mrs. Dobbs?"

"Call me Judy. Call me anything." Judy was trying not to show her panic. She found the door and felt the wood. "It isn't hot," she thought. "There's still time."

"Let's go, Judy! Mamma may be worrying about me. Cousin Charlie said the danger was all over and Mamma wouldn't have to watch me any more. That's why I went with him. And then Liz came, and it was so cozy here telling stories and all. But I remember now. Liz was crying, and it wasn't a sad story . . ."

"Oh, it is! It is! It's the saddest story I ever lived

through," Judy was thinking. Tears were rolling down her cheeks. She knew just how Liz felt. Rosita chattered on, confident that everything would be all right, until she turned the doorknob.

"It's locked!" she exclaimed. "Did you know it was locked, Judy?"

"Yes, Rosita, I knew. Your cousin Vin locked it. Do you think you can persuade him to open it?"

"Not now. He's busy burning papers."

"Maybe we can break it then. It's old wood. Let's try," Judy suggested.

"How will we do it?"

Rosita was eager to help. Judy felt around in the dark and found a loose baseboard. A nail tore into her arm, leaving a long scratch. She ignored it as she ripped the board loose.

"There!" she exclaimed. "We'll use this as a battering ram the way the police do when they have to break into a house."

"We aren't breaking in," Rosita objected. "We're breaking out. We have to break out on account of the fire. Judy, couldn't the firemen help us?"

"There's no way to call them. Unless somebody sees the fire—"

Rosita raised herself on the window sill.

"I don't see it myself any more, but I can still smell the smoke. Maybe we won't have to break down the door."

"We do have to, Rosita. It's the only way."

"Won't the police arrest us for breaking a door?"

"No, of course not. I wish they'd come!"

"The police?" Rosita questioned in amazement. "Judy, aren't you afraid of them?"

"Afraid of the police!" Judy exclaimed. "Of course not. I wish they were here now. They'd get us out of this room fast."

"Can't we get ourselves out?"

"We can try. You take hold of this end of the board. Watch out for nails! And when I say *run*, we'll both run as hard as we can and bang the board against that locked door. I think it will open. Let's try it and see."

Rosita hesitated, groping around in the dark and trying to get a firm hold on her end of the board.

"I have it," she announced at last. "It doesn't matter if we spoil the house, does it? They're going to tear it down, anyway."

"That's right," Judy agreed. "The house doesn't matter, but we do. Ready? *Run!*"

CHAPTER XXI

Just in Time

THERE was a great crash and a splintering of wood. At the same time something hit Judy so hard it stunned her for a moment. Staggering to her feet, she felt the door to see what had happened. The panels were intact. It was the board they had been using as a battering ram that had broken.

"We can't get out. Cousin Vin! Please! Let us out!" screamed Rosita, suddenly aware of their predicament. "They did this because Papa wouldn't pay," she said, beginning to sob. "Mamma was right. She said something would happen!"

"Listen!" Judy exclaimed. "Isn't that a truck driving away?"

"They took the machines back. That's what they did," sobbed Rosita. "Their old money machines are more important than we are!"

"I'm afraid you're right, Rosita. They have taken the machines." Judy listened. "I don't hear that crackling noise any more, do you?"

"No, but I hear something else! It's a siren. It doesn't sound much like fire engines."

"It's the police!" exclaimed Judy. "They'll get us out! Maybe Peter is with them. Oh, I wish I could see! I can hear them out there, can't you? They've stopped that truck!"

"They won't let Cousin Vin take away those money machines, will they?"

"They certainly won't!" Judy declared. "And they won't leave us in here very long, either. We'd better yell good and loud so they'll know where we are. Did you ever hear a yell like this?" And Judy shouted at the top of her lungs: "*Hip deminiga folliga sock de bump de lolliga yoo hoo!*"

Rosita joined in on the "*Yoo hoo!*"

"Peter will know that yell," Judy explained when the echo had faded. "We used to yell it when we were playing hide-and-seek. Listen!"

From far away came an answering yell. Judy giggled as she thought of Peter's dignified companions in the police car staring at him in amazement. She didn't know what they'd think of what she'd done.

But if she hadn't done it, Peter might have waited until morning and then it might have been too late. Already the first flush of daylight showed through the little square that was their window.

"Rosita, they're coming up here," Judy said, releasing the night latch. "They will be policemen in uniform. Don't be afraid of them."

"Is your husband in the FBI?" Rosita asked. "Liz said he was."

"Liz was right. But don't be frightened. He carries a gun for your protection—and mine. It's a very different kind of protection than what they wanted your father to pay."

"Judy?" a voice called from the other side of the door as the bolt slid back. "I thought I'd find you here," Peter said as he strode into the room. "Is Mr. Rocklin's little girl with you?"

"She is. Oh, Peter!" Judy exclaimed. "I knew you'd come. You just had to come. Vincent Norton locked me in here with Rosita. He was going to make it look like an accident."

"What happens to him will be no accident!" Peter declared savagely. "He will pay for this, and so will all the others—"

"Not Charlie," Rosita protested. "Please, not Cousin Charlie. He and Liz were so good to me."

Peter gave Judy a puzzled glance. Then, all tenderness, he took her in his arms and kissed her.

It was at this point that a burly policeman arrived on the scene and said to the group of men who came up behind him, "I guess Dobbs found what he was looking for, all right. Now it's your turn, Mr. Rocklin. I told you we'd see that your little girl wasn't harmed."

"Papa!" cried Rosita, throwing herself at him and hugging him so hard he couldn't speak. Finally, releasing her hold a little, she asked, "Where's Mamma? Was she worried?"

"Your Mamma won't talk to me. It is all my fault, she says. You are already dead. But you are not dead!"

"How silly you are," Rosita said, kissing her father again. "I couldn't be kissing you if I were dead, could I?" She looked at Judy gratefully and said, "It is because of her that you found me, Papa. She told the police—"

"No," objected Peter. "She told only your father and me. He told the police, at my suggestion, and now he has the best protection in the world. He's promised to cooperate with us to the fullest, and do you know why? Because this little redheaded wife of mine had courage enough to drive off in the night to a row of empty houses and look for you."

"I would have followed," Mr. Rocklin said, "but my car had been tampered with. The wires had been torn out so I could not start it."

"I see." Judy was glad to hear that his intentions had been good. "Instead, Vincent Norton followed me.

He was burning something downstairs. We thought he was trying to set the house on fire. Let's go down and see what he was burning."

They were all glad to follow Judy's suggestion.

Downstairs, under the brilliance of police torches, she soon discovered what it was that Vincent Norton had been burning. It was the contents of that wastebasket. But Peter was not discouraged. "I'll take this to the lab. We'll soon find out what it was he was afraid to have us find."

"It might have been this." Judy opened her pocketbook to show him the crumpled paper. It was spread out on the table while everybody gathered around to study the map and read off the names.

"This gives us the whole picture," one policeman commented. "What a racket!"

Judy could see what he meant. On the paper were the names of different members of the criminal syndicate and the businesses they controlled, not in Washington, but in Chicago. The floor plan was of a Chicago café.

"That's the way they work it!" Mr. Rocklin shouted, suddenly excited. "That could be my motel. They take for laundry, for glasses, for cigarette machines, ice dispensers, everything! And now they want me to put in one of these!"

He pointed to one lone gambling machine the men evidently had not had time to load into the truck.

"These things are legal in a few states. More federal controls would make them illegal all over the country," Peter said, "but you can't enforce a law until the people are ready for it. That's where Senator Hockett is going to run into trouble. If his bill is going to deprive the states of their rights—"

"His bill," the burly policeman interrupted Peter, "will be passed if the people want it. We'll drive you and your little girl home, Mr. Rocklin. It's our job, from now on, to see that no harm comes to her."

"Wait, Papa!" Rosita cried. "Charlie said I could watch the machines tear down the houses. It's morning now, and the wreckers must be coming. Can't we stay and watch?"

There were tears in Mr. Rocklin's eyes as he answered gruffly, "No! You mind your papa. We'll go home now. Another day we'll come back and watch."

"That's one sight I *don't* want to see," Judy said, snuggling close to Peter in their own car going home. "I may as well tell you, I was scared pink—"

"As pink as that sky?" Peter pointed out the sunrise, which looked like a picture postcard over the Capitol, tinting the statue of Freedom with rosy colors. Morning had never seemed so beautiful.

Peter was not taking the roundabout route, but the most direct road home. Maryland Avenue proved to be only a few short blocks from the condemned area around the row of empty houses. Peter drove on past the Capitol and the Supreme Court Building with its noble motto: EQUAL JUSTICE UNDER LAW. Judy gazed at the tall Corinthian columns and read: JUSTICE, THE GUARDIAN OF LIBERTY, as Peter drove around the building. They skirted another one of those confusing parks with a statue in the center, and in a surprisingly short time they were back at the motel.

"You look tired," Judy said, noticing how red Peter's eyes were. "Did you get any sleep?"

"Not a wink," he replied. "Did you?"

"Only a cat nap before I started." She stopped herself. "I shouldn't mention cats, should I? We didn't find Blackberry. Every time I enter this room I think of the way we left him—"

"And I think of his collar tucked in that cash drawer. I'm determined to get the truth out of Walter Krut," declared Peter.

"Vincent Norton worked for him. I can tell you that much."

"Well, I can tell him something. That job is finished, and any work Charlie did for him on the side is all over, too. Krut's Rotisserie is closed up for good. Walter Krut is still in jail, and the charges that are piling up against him will keep him behind bars for a long time. We have definite proof now, thanks to that whisper you heard, that he belongs to an international crime syndicate," Peter finished. "You'll read about it in the morning papers."

CHAPTER XXII

The Invisible Government

JUDY did not see the morning papers until late in the afternoon. She and Peter had both taken a day off to catch up on lost sleep. Now, refreshed and ready for anything, it was obvious that there was much yet to be done. The headlines in the morning papers proclaimed:

Whisper overheard in Statuary Hall and reported to the FBI late yesterday starts new investigation into the activities of a nationwide criminal syndicate . . .

Judy read on. It surprised her that no names were mentioned except those of criminals already convicted.

Actually, the news item was little more than a recital of criminal activities in the past.

"Because the FBI has to deal with such people, our investigations have to be secret. You can understand that," Peter said.

"Of course. I see why wives are supposed to keep out of them, too. We might do more harm than good. But Peter, I had to go to that empty house. I had to go before it was too late."

"I'm not blaming you for that, Angel. It was a courageous thing to do. You should receive some recognition—"

"I don't want it from anyone but you," Judy stopped him. "Names in the paper aren't important. Ideas are. I think everybody will get the idea that Senator Hockett is putting up a real fight against what he calls 'the invisible government of crime.' It scares me just to read about it. And when I think how close we came, Rosita and I, to being victims—"

"You'll testify to that before the senate committee?"

"Gladly. I'll testify to everything, and I think Liz would, too, except that she can't testify against her husband. Naturally, she wants her Charlie to get off with as light a sentence as possible. Peter," Judy asked curiously, "did you find out what his business is?"

Peter shook his head. There was a lot he still hadn't found out. The investigation was going on in secret. Names were kept secret for the protection of innocent

people like the Rocklins, who refused to press kid-
napping charges against either Vincent Norton or
Charlie. The FBI, of course, would hold both Norton
and Charlie on extortion charges.

"He took Charlie to that empty house and made
him stay there with Rosita," Liz told Judy that evening.
"He was locked in, Judy, just the way you were. It
was Vincent Norton who opened the door for me, not
Charlie," Liz went on. "He forced us to leave after
Rosita went to sleep, but Charlie intended to sneak
back there and save her, Judy. I know he did. He
told her they'd both be watching from a safe distance
when the houses were torn down."

"I believe you, Liz," Judy said sympathetically.

The two of them sat in a secluded corner of the
lobby talking. Liz was one of those being questioned
indirectly by Peter. Actually Judy did most of the
questioning and then reported the answers. That, she
discovered, was one way she could really help. A girl
would confide in another girl more quickly than in a
government agent. It was only when she asked about
Blackberry that Liz averted her face.

"I tell you I don't know where your cat is. I wish
I did. I really would like to help you find him, Judy,"
she declared warmly.

She sounded sincere, and yet Judy was puzzled. Liz
knew something she wasn't telling. That guilty expression on her face gave her away.

"Have you seen what it said in the papers?" Liz asked after an uncomfortable silence.

Judy had seen. The evening papers carried more of the story. Vincent Norton and Walter Krut were being charged with conspiracy against the government. One of two unnamed men, the news report said, had been seized with Vincent Norton by the FBI and local police in a condemned building on F Street where a meeting of the conspirators appeared to have taken place. The three men, including Walter Krut, were ordered to appear before the Federal Grand Jury. Judy and Peter would be there, and so would Liz.

"I can tell the Grand Jury exactly how the crime syndicate took over Charlie's business," she declared. "It was an honest selling job at first. But the next thing Charlie knew he was selling things he didn't even know were hidden in his company's products."

"What were their products?" Judy asked curiously.

Liz told her they manufactured hotel equipment and novelties. "By the time Charlie realized what was going on," Liz continued, "he was in so deep, he was afraid to back out."

Judy nodded. "I heard Vincent Norton ordering Charlie to make something look like an accident," she said.

"He said Vin threatened him," Liz agreed.

"I believe that," affirmed Judy. "His voice sounded

threatening enough. It frightened me and I started to run. That was when I encountered the laundry machine ghost. It did look weird, but after my experience in those empty houses I doubt if I'll ever be frightened by anything like that again."

"If you were frightened, can you imagine how I felt? Vin saw that his orders were obeyed or else." Liz paused for emphasis, then continued, "Charlie went along with them at first. You know how it is. You tell yourself everybody else is doing it and so it's all right, but you know in your heart it isn't."

"I know," Judy sympathized. "Liz, think about the future instead. It can be bright for both you and Charlie. Peter says he probably won't receive a long sentence unless— I mean," Judy amended, not wanting to put it too bluntly, "as long as no real harm comes to Senator Hockett. It's that one man who worries me. He's still free. He may try to carry out their original plan."

"Do you know who he is, Judy?"

"No, do you?"

Liz shook her head. "Charlie doesn't know either. He saw the two of them, of course. But so did you."

"Only briefly." Judy tried her best to remember as much as she could about those other two men. They both had dark hair. She remembered that much. And one shuffled his feet when he walked, as if his shoes were too big for him.

It wasn't much of a description, but it seemed to be enough to satisfy Senator Hockett later in the week when Judy called to see him in his office across Constitution Avenue from the Capitol. She didn't cross the street in the regular way. She wanted to ride that queer little subway that had been built especially for senators. She wanted to explore the basement of the Old Senate Office Building, too.

"This is where Blackberry was supposed to catch mice," she thought sadly as she waited for the subway.

Senators and tourists crowded in, and the subway was soon on its way. It reminded Judy of a toy railroad in an amusement park except that it had a serious purpose. It took busy senators from their offices to the Senate Chamber and back again. It saved time. Judy knew how important that was.

"There's so little time to find that man," she told Senator Hockett when, at last, she was ushered into his office by his pleasant young secretary.

The senator refused to believe he was in any danger. "Secret Service men guard me so closely, I have no privacy," he complained. "What bothers me is this. How could anyone know the words I plan to use when I introduce my bill? I have no ghost writers. I have not dictated the speech. I have not written it down. And the only time I ever practice it is when I am alone."

"Here in the office?" Judy questioned, looking

around the rather ornate room and discovering an eagle exactly like the one on the wall of their motel room.

"Yes, and at home. As I said before, unless someone can read my mind—"

Judy glanced up at the eagle.

"Maybe a little bird told on you," she suggested.

CHAPTER XXIII

Soul Liberty

"A LITTLE BIRD?" Senator Hockett followed Judy's glance. "Do you mean that eagle?"

"Yes, he's hollow. Did you know? There's an eagle just like him in our room at the Eagle Motel. We took it apart and found a hollow place inside. I was just thinking," Judy said. "There's room enough behind that eagle's beak to hide a small recorder. Maybe somebody 'bugged' your office."

"But why? Why would anyone want to record what is said in this office unless— That's it!" he exclaimed, jumping up from his chair. "I do have enemies. The invisible government of crime in this country would like nothing better than to worm its way into politics."

He jerked down the eagle and snapped it open. "You're right. A recorder of some kind could have been hidden in here. But if so, it's been removed. Who had access to it?"

"Who cleans your office?" Judy asked.

The name of the man who did the waxing turned out to be Oscar Ceron. This would have meant nothing to Judy if she hadn't remembered that Ceron was one of the names written on the crumpled map she had found in the wastebasket back in the empty house.

"This ought to be reported right now," she told the senator. "There's a Ceron connected, somehow, with the protection racket. Maybe this man is his brother or something."

"They're all brothers. This invisible government of crime has been called the Brotherhood of Evil and not without reason. They could take over our country if we sat back and let them. Who knows how many of these little birds are planted in various offices?" Senator Hockett remained thoughtful for a moment. Then he said, "I do remember receiving this eagle as a gift. The giver should be investigated."

"When my husband comes in, I wish you'd tell him about it," Judy suggested. "He may go eagle hunting for you."

The eagle hunt was soon organized. Senator Hockett had plenty to tell Peter when he came in. They talked and talked. Among the things discussed was his bill which would come before the Senate on Friday or Monday at the very latest. Recent publicity had made it more popular. Now the public knew how the racketeers moved in on honest businesses like Mr. Rocklin's motel. Vincent Norton and his criminal employer had collected most of Mr. Rocklin's profits along with the profits from a great many other businesses. The money thus raised went to finance crime and keep top criminals safe in their country estates.

"There are known to be several such estates in your part of Pennsylvania," the senator continued. "Here, let me show you."

He brought out a map of the eastern part of the United States. It was divided into the territories controlled by various gangsters. They operated within the law as far as anybody knew. It was their secret business that was the concern of the senator and of every American, he declared heatedly.

"Maybe you couldn't give me a cat to catch the mice in the Capitol basement, but you've helped smoke out these rats and that's more important!" he said.

"Don't you have any cats in the basement?" Judy questioned. "I didn't see any—"

"You wouldn't see them. They keep out of the way," Senator Hockett replied with one of his famous smiles. "There's a calico and a yellow female and one big black male, a lovable cat if I ever saw one. A Secret Service agent found him trapped inside one of those grottos just west of the Capitol—"

"He did? When?" Judy asked excitedly.

"Let me see? It was the very day you offered me your pet. I didn't think of it then. It couldn't be the same cat, could it?"

Judy's thoughts flew back to that faint cry she had heard. She had blamed it on a catbird.

"I didn't know Blackberry was gone then, but I suppose someone could have dropped him inside that grotto. There were four small openings near the top. Maybe that's why Liz wanted to walk that way. Then she discovered the slab had been removed and Blackberry was gone, so she was afraid to tell me. And all the time he's been living here in the Capitol and catching mice just the way we wanted him to!"

"Better make sure he's your cat before you get too excited," Senator Hockett advised. "He had no collar."

Judy explained about the collar Peter had found. When Liz was questioned later, she admitted that Charlie had been instructed by Walter Krut to get rid of the cat and had dropped him inside the grotto.

"I wanted to tell you, but I was afraid," Liz explained. "You see, I thought your cat was really lost, and I didn't want you to blame Charlie. But it's all right now," she added. "Mr. Rocklin says you can keep the cat here at the motel if you like."

"No," Judy objected, "he can serve his country better at the Capitol. We saw him there, but we didn't let him see us for fear we'd make him homesick. But when we do go home, Blackberry goes along."

"I'm glad." Liz hesitated. "Maybe I was wrong about Senator Hockett. If he introduces his bill tomorrow, I'd like to be there."

"We'll go together. Peter can't sit with me, and I do want to be there. We can investigate that whisper, too," Judy added. "It was so strange, and yet it must be quite commonplace. Everyone who takes the tour talks about it. Even Rosita—"

"Shall we take her with us, Judy? If that man should show up, she could point him out better than anyone."

Judy thought it was an excellent idea to take Rosita. It would be easy to get additional passes. To Judy's surprise, Mrs. Rocklin did not object.

"You watch her good," she cautioned Judy. "But you saved my Rosita. I have not forgotten. I know you'll keep her safe."

"I will, Mrs. Rocklin. You'll see!"

Rosita was excited about her second tour of the Capitol, but she was a little afraid, too. "If I do see that man—"

"Just act as if you didn't. Pinch me, and I'll know."

"Pinch you?"

"Yes, hard, so it hurts. You see," Judy explained, "they had a plan—"

"Like that plan to make the house fall on us?"

"Something like that. Only this time it isn't us they

want to hurt. It's Senator Hockett, because he wants a new law that will make it easier for the federal government to control crime. He's going to talk about it in the Senate this morning."

"And I'm going to hear him? When do we start?" asked Rosita, suddenly eager to go.

Later she sat very quietly in the Senate gallery between Judy and Liz. She hadn't seen anyone who looked remotely like the missing conspirator.

"I guess he's given up the idea of hurting Senator Hockett," she whispered.

"I hope so," Judy whispered back. "There's the senator now, smiling as usual."

He was ready to make his speech. All eyes turned toward him as he began: "I need not tell you, honored Vice President and gentlemen of the Senate, that the invisible government of crime in our beloved country is a serious threat to our cherished ideals of freedom and democracy. And when I say freedom I do not mean what the criminal means when he says, 'This is a free country,' believing it to be free for him to follow his own selfish purposes without regard for the rights or even the lives of his fellow citizens. What I am talking about is freedom to do what an educated conscience tells us is right not only for ourselves but for all people. This is true soul liberty . . ."

A slight movement back of Judy and a sudden pinch on her arm made her realize Senator Hockett had used the fateful words. A little man two rows behind them had removed a fountain pen from his pocket. But before he could raise his hand, the deadly pen had been whisked out of it by a Secret Service agent who quickly subdued him after a short, violent scuffle.

"He's the one!" Rosita was whispering excitedly. "The one who shuffled his feet!"

Now Judy recognized him, too. He was removed from the Senate gallery quietly while Senator Hockett continued his speech. It was short and to the point. Investigators of nationwide crime should no longer operate on a temporary basis, he said, but should receive permanent status through congressional legislation.

All this would take time. The bill would be discussed, possibly for weeks, in the Senate before it went to the House of Representatives where more discussion would take place. The President could veto it if he saw fit. But now the complex machinery of a free government had been set in motion, and Judy had been there to watch it. Never, as long as she lived, would she forget Senator Hockett's face as he pronounced the brave words: *Soul Liberty*.

"I'll let them be my watchword," she resolved.

CHAPTER XXIV

Reassured!

JUDY was alone on one side of Statuary Hall. But this time the statues did not frighten her. Liz, Rosita, and a dozen or more tourists taking the guided tour were on the other side, listening. Judy whispered something very low.

"We can't hear you," the guide called. "Stand on the brass plate and try it again."

Looking down at her feet, Judy saw that one of the tiles was marked with a shining piece of brass. She stood on it, leaning forward a little, and whispered again, "Soul Liberty is my watchword."

Then she crossed the floor quickly. Strangers were smiling at her as if they were old friends. Tourists in

Washington were like that. Judy was finding the nation's capital a very friendly place.

"We heard that all right. Does anyone else want to try it?" the guide asked.

One after another they heard the whisper that had seemed so mysterious to Judy. Many of them borrowed her watchword. But since she had borrowed it from Senator Hockett and he had borrowed it from Roger Williams, Judy said she didn't mind. Words like that were meant to be uttered down through the ages.

"He called himself a seeker," someone said, and Judy took the words to heart. She would call herself a seeker, too. Right now she was seeking the answer to that mysterious whisper and, happily, finding it.

"This hall was originally the Hall of Representatives," the guide explained, "but as the nation grew, the hall became too small to accommodate its members. Those who sat in the front gallery were hemmed in so completely that they were unable to leave for refreshments."

"How tragic!" several people commented.

It was good to hear laughter echoing through the solemn hall, even though Judy fancied the statues seemed to disapprove.

"What did they do for something to eat?" a small boy questioned.

"Refreshments were passed up to them on long

sticks," the guide replied. "Such crowded conditions made an extension necessary. And so, in 1859, our Representatives moved into the present Hall which is the largest legislative chamber in the world. The acoustics was another reason for the move."

"Will you explain that, please?" asked Judy. "I know my whisper could be heard across the hall, but I still don't understand why."

The guide tried to explain it, pointing out the peculiar shape of the domed ceiling and telling an amusing story about the congressman who used to sit where the brass plate was now.

"People couldn't understand why he kept interrupting the proceedings," she finished. "If he cleared his throat or made the slightest sound it was mistaken for an interruption. It was really quite embarrassing."

"It's still a little mysterious," Judy said, and the others taking the tour agreed with her.

"It trapped Charlie," Liz whispered, pulling Judy aside. "Did you know your husband and another FBI agent followed him and picked him up right after I tried so hard to make you understand? I should be sorry he got caught, but I'm not. This separation will give us both a little time to grow up. I'll be waiting for him, Judy. Maybe he was weak, but so was I. Meeting you made all the difference. There's one thing that hasn't changed, though. I still love him."

"I'm glad. He's going to need your love," Judy said in a half whisper.

This was a confidence between them. Liz was like Honey in many ways. Soon the two of them would meet. Judy had telephoned home and invited Peter's sister to Washington for the week end. Judy and Peter were going to be there at least another week for the hearings. But it would be a pleasant week. There was so much to see and learn that a whole summer in Washington wouldn't have been too long.

"We'll tour the White House and all those museums and see the tomb of the unknown soldier. I haven't used my pass for the House of Representatives yet, or seen the sub-basement where Blackberry goes hunting. Imagine it, Liz!" exclaimed Judy. "He was here in the United States Capitol all the time we were so worried about him. If he'd had his collar on—"

"Walter Krut must have removed it before he gave him to us. There are some people who can't resist stealing anything made of gold, and Walter Krut is one of them." Liz sighed. "Charlie trusted him, and we all trusted Cousin Vin. This is going to be hard on his wife."

"You can make it easier."

"I'll try. You've done me so much good, Judy. I had a choice to make, and you helped me decide on the right one."

Her eyes followed Rosita as she spoke. They were touring the Hall of Columns where a few of the heavier statues had been moved to keep Statuary Hall from being too crowded and also to distribute the weight, the guide said. Rosita was looking at the various statues and reading off the names.

In the architect's office Judy was given a booklet which contained brief biographies of the men who had been honored by their states.

"I was curious about Uriah M. Rose. Let's look him up and see who he was," she suggested.

She found his name under Arkansas.

"He was an ambassador of peace for Theodore Roosevelt in 1907. Now let's look up somebody else."

"Wait!" Rosita's hand stopped Judy's as she was about to turn the page. "You didn't look up the name of the sculptor. See! It's F. W. Ruckstull. Maybe I'll be an artist or a sculptor when I grow up. Do you think that's a good idea?" Rosita asked.

Judy told her she thought it was a fine idea. "Honey is an artist. You'll meet her tomorrow. I want to look my very best when she comes. I think I'll have my hair washed and set in the beauty parlor downstairs."

Back at the motel that evening Judy had to tell Peter all about her exciting day. They had dinner at one of the outdoor tables while they talked.

"The whisper was still mysterious even after the guide explained it, and those statues still seem almost alive," Judy confessed.

"Did you whisper your own private watchword? You said you would. What was it?" Peter asked.

"It was the same as Senator Hockett's. Afterwards

I went downstairs and had my hair done. And who do you suppose sat in my lap all the time I was in the beauty parlor?"

"I hope it was Blackberry!"

"It was. Oh, Peter! It was so good to hold him again. He acted proud of himself just as if he *knew*."

"Knew what?" Peter questioned when Judy paused.

"Just that we all have a part," she explained. "Even cats can serve their country if it's as good a country as this one. I keep thinking about what Senator Hockett said. I never thought of a conscience as being educated before, did you? But I guess he's right. Little babies aren't born knowing right from wrong. They have to be taught."

"Sometimes they have to learn the hard way," Peter commented. "Charlie is the only one of all those I questioned who was willing to cooperate with us. I'm afraid we'll have to reeducate his conscience, though. He learned too much from Vincent Norton and Walter Krut. Krut is wanted for a long series of crimes."

Judy was quiet for a moment, finishing her dessert. Her gray eyes were thoughtful as if she could see into the future where another mystery, THE SECRET QUEST, was waiting to be solved.

A little later, when Judy and Peter had finished dinner and were taking a walk around the enclosed court, Rosita danced up to them. She reminded Judy of a bird just learning to fly. The mother bird was no longer watching. Now she must depend on her own wings.

"It's been a beautiful day," she sang out. "I'm on my way to change into my bathing suit. Will you join me in the pool?"

"Why not?" Judy's eyes met Peter's. "Wasn't it the pool that attracted us to this motel in the first place?"

"Was it?" asked Peter. "I thought the eagles—"

Judy made a face at him. "You know they're only symbols. You were the one who was attracted to them."

But she was beginning to understand why.